J. E. Vernon

Bible Truths in Simple Words

short addresses to children

J. E. Vernon

Bible Truths in Simple Words
short addresses to children

ISBN/EAN: 9783337361181

Printed in Europe, USA, Canada, Australia, Japan

Cover: Foto ©Andreas Hilbeck / pixelio.de

More available books at **www.hansebooks.com**

𝔅𝔦𝔟𝔩𝔢 𝔗𝔯𝔲𝔱𝔥𝔰 𝔦𝔫 𝔖𝔦𝔪𝔭𝔩𝔢 𝔚𝔬𝔯𝔡𝔰.

SHORT ADDRESSES TO CHILDREN.

BY THE

REV. J. E. VERNON,

VICAR OF BICKNOLLER. SOMERSET.

LONDON:

J. MASTERS AND CO., 78, NEW BOND STREET.

MDCCCLXXVIL

LONDON :

J. MASTERS AND CO., PRINTERS,

ALBION BUILDINGS, BARTHOLOMEW CLOSE, E.C.

Bible Truths in Simple Words.

I.

THE OMNIPRESENCE OF GOD.

" Thou God seest me."—Gen. xvi. 13.

SARAH, Abraham's wife, had an Egyptian maidservant named Hagar. Now, when Abraham and Sarah were very old and yet had no children, Sarah persuaded Abraham to marry Hagar. This was very wrong; for GOD had promised Abraham a son, and, although Abraham had faith to believe it at the time, he had not faith enough to wait patiently for GOD to perform His promise. It was very wrong, too, for Abraham to take another wife, and even though his own wife Sarah wished him to do it, he ought not to have listened to her. No doubt it was very hard for him to resist the temptation when his own dear wife was the tempter, and his own impatience made him inclined to welcome her advice; and although he was a good man and feared GOD and trusted in Him, yet we must remember that he had been brought up in idolatry, and had only

B

lately learned to know the true GOD. So we must not be surprised if we read that he sometimes did wrong. Even good Christian people who know much more about GOD than Abraham did then, sometimes give way to temptation, and do what they ought not to do. When we are tempted to do anything wrong, even if our dearest friend persuades us, and our own hearts incline us to it, we should think of GOD's eye upon us, and say, "How can I do this great wickedness, and sin against GOD?" Well, Abraham listened to his wife and married Hagar, and the consequence was that his home soon became very unhappy. Hagar was impudent to her mistress, and Sarah went and blamed Abraham for having done just what she had herself persuaded him to do. So people often act. They persuade others to do wrong, and then, when trouble comes, instead of taking the blame to themselves, they lay it upon others, perhaps upon the very person whom they had led wrong.

Abraham would not shelter Hagar from her mistress's anger, but told Sarah to do what she liked with her maid. And Sarah treated Hagar so harshly that she ran away from her. Hagar was making her way back to Egypt, and was by a fountain of water in the wilderness, when GOD sent an angel to her. The angel told her to go back to her mistress, and submit herself under her hands, and at the same time comforted her by the promise of a son who should be a famous man and father of a great nation. Now Hagar seems to have been rather surprised that GOD had seen her even in the wilderness. No doubt she had heard of the true GOD from Abraham and Sarah, but she had been brought up in Egypt, and had been accustomed to believe that there were many gods, and that one had power in one place, another in another. So very likely she thought that in running away from Abraham and Sarah she was also leaving behind her the GOD whom they worshipped. When she found, then, that GOD saw her even in that lonely place, she was full of wonder, and called Him by a name which in our language means "Thou GOD seest me."

Now, I want you to remember these four simple words always all through life, "Thou GOD seest me." You can never go anywhere where GOD is not. You can never do anything or suffer anything which GOD does not see. You can never say anything which GOD does not hear. You can never think anything which GOD did not know even before it entered your mind. David felt this. He wrote, "O LORD, Thou knowest my down-sitting, and mine uprising; Thou understandest my thoughts long before. Thou art about my path and about my bed, and spiest out all my ways. For lo, there is not a word in my tongue, but Thou, O LORD, knowest it altogether." "Whither shall I go, then, from Thy SPIRIT, or whither shall I go then from Thy Presence? If I climb up into heaven, Thou art there : if I go down to hell,"—that is Hades, the resting-place of departed spirits,—"Thou art there also. If I take the wings of the morning, and remain in the uttermost parts of the sea, even there also shall Thy hand lead me and Thy right hand shall hold me. If I say, Peradventure the darkness shall cover me, then shall my night be turned to day. Yea, the darkness is no darkness with Thee, but the night is as clear as the day; the darkness and light to Thee are both alike." A child was once asked if he could tell where GOD was, and was offered an orange if he could tell. "Tell me," said he to his questioner, "where GOD is not, and I will give you two." I read once of a girl who went into her master's room—a room not much frequented—to steal. There was a portrait in the room, and the eyes of the portrait seemed to follow her wherever she went. This made her uneasy, so, to get rid of those eyes, she took down the portrait and cut the eyes out. If she could have plucked out GOD's eye, she might have sinned without fear; but so long as GOD's eye was upon her, it was a vain thing that the eyes of the portrait could follow her no more. It has been well said of Moses, who before he slew the Egyptian looked this way and that way; that if he had looked *up*, he would never have killed him. The thought of those words, "Thou GOD seest me," would keep us from many a sin. But I do not want you to think of this merely as a thought to frighten you. It *ought* to make you afraid to do anything wrong. But I want it to be a thought to encourage you to do right. You know a soldier fights all the more bravely when he knows that the eye of his officer is upon him observing his courage. There is a story in the Gospels of a poor widow who put into the treasury of GOD's temple at Jerusalem a very small sum, about a farthing. It was all she had, and I dare say it was a hard struggle to part with it. She did not know who was watching her. But JESUS saw her little gift, knew what it cost her, and He has taken care that

that poor widow's self-denying offering should be known all over the world, and never be forgotten. And He notices still, and never will forget, every good and kind and self-denying action of the poorest person and of the smallest child. Take care, dear children, to hide as much as you can from the eyes of men what you give or do in kindness for CHRIST's sake, and "your FATHER who seeth in secret shall reward you openly." Fight bravely against every temptation to do wrong, and though no human eye can see the inward struggle or know how much the effort cost you, let it be encouragement to know that your FATHER in heaven has seen it all.

Then, the time may come when you shall be in trouble or pain, and then the thought, " Thou GOD seest me," will be full of comfort. Jonah was in great trouble in the fish's belly down in the depths of the sea, but he knew that even there GOD could see him, and help him. So he cried to GOD in his fear and trouble, and GOD heard him and delivered him. The disciples were overtaken by a furious storm on the lake, and they were frightened and tugged at the oars, but could make no head against the great waves, and they could not think what had become of JESUS. But His eye was upon them all the time, and by-and-by He came to them over the waters with His cheering words, "It is I, be not afraid ;" and as soon as He came into the boat they were in peace and safety. Remember, then, in the time of fear or trouble, or pain, JESUS sees you, knows all you suffer, feels for you, and will help you if you call upon Him.

And if you have, unhappily, done wrong, still do

not be afraid to think, " Thou GOD seest me." It did not make the Prodigal Son afraid because his father had seen him act so wickedly. It made him very *sorry;* but instead of being frightened to seek his father's forgiveness, he went to him and said, " Father, I have sinned against heaven, and *in thy sight.*" And when S. Peter had denied JESUS before men, he was not *afraid* when he saw the eye of JESUS fixed upon him ; but he was very, very sorry, and went out all by himself and wept bitterly. It cut him to the heart, but it did not frighten him. So, my dear children, when you are tempted to do wrong, let the thought of GOD's eye check you. When you have an opportunity of doing a good and kind act, do it in the faith that GOD is noticing it with the approving eye of a FATHER who sees His child trying to do what will please Him. When you are in danger, or think you are, remember Who is about your path and about your bed. You are safe under His protection. If you are in pain or trouble, lift up your heart to JESUS, Who suffered dreadful pain for you, and be sure that He knows all, and cares for you. If you have done wrong, think of those saddened eyes which were dimmed with blood and tears for you upon the cross, and be sorry, oh, be sorry, but do not be afraid to tell Him all and ask Him to forgive you.

II.

OUR FATHER'S GIFT.

" Fear not, little flock; for it is your Father's good pleasure to give you the kingdom."—S. Luke xii. 32.

THESE are the words of JESUS CHRIST, the Good Shepherd, and they are for you. For you are part of His little flock, you are His lambs, the objects of His special care. And He tells you here of your FATHER'S love for you, and of the splendid present which He offers you, and of the pleasure it gives Him to bestow it on you. GOD, your heavenly FATHER, loves you very much for His dear SON'S sake, who loved you and gave Himself for you. And so, because JESUS died for you and bought you with the price of His precious blood, GOD has taken you to be His children. At your baptism you were made members of CHRIST, and therefore children of GOD and inheritors of the kingdom of heaven.

Now I want you to think, first, what a great thing it is to have such a FATHER. If a child has an earthly father who is very rich, and has a grand house and park and a great many servants under him, that child feels very proud of such a father. But all the world belongs to GOD, and thousands of worlds besides this, and heaven is His house and all the angels are His servants, and if you had wings and could fly far away thousands of miles beyond the farthest star you could never go out of the dominions of GOD's kingdom. All is GOD's, and GOD is your FATHER. See, then,

how rich and great your FATHER is ! And then think
how powerful He is ! He had only to speak and the
world was made. He made the glorious sun and the
moon and all the stars. He made every tree and flower,
every fish and bird and living thing. And He made
us, and fearfully and wonderfully we are made, made
in the image and likeness of GOD. In a moment He
could destroy all that He has made. He could take
away our breath, and we should die. He is your almighty FATHER. You know that an earthly father
may be very great, and rich, and powerful, and be
able to do a great many things for his dear children,
but if any of his children fall ill, he cannot make them
well. He may call in the most skilful doctors, but
they cannot make them well. But GOD can either make
them well or not, as He sees best. Sometimes He
hears their parents' prayers, and blesses the medicines
which the doctor gives, and gives the sick child his
health again. Sometimes He sees it best to take the
little one away from troubles to come, and to call it
away to His beautiful paradise to be more happy than
it could ever be on earth. He is as wise as He is
powerful, and always does what is kindest and best.
For GOD, your FATHER, is not only all-rich and almighty and all-wise. He is also all Love. And He
loves you so much that He will use all His riches and
power and wisdom for your good and happiness, if
you will let Him—that is, if you will believe that He
loves you, and will trust His wisdom, and try to
do what He tells you. And He only tells you to
do what is really best for your happiness, and not
to do what would be sure to make you unhappy.

Do you ask how you are to know that He loves you and cares for your happiness so much? Well, think of this. Suppose you had behaved very badly and ungratefully to some one, and that a great trouble came upon you, and some wicked people were to carry you off to be a slave in some far-off land, and your friends could not help you or persuade those cruel people by any offers of money to let you go. And then suppose that this person whom you had treated so ill were to hear of your distress, and send his only son to be a slave in your stead, and so you were set free, but that good man's son were to suffer horrible ill-treatment and to be put to a cruel death in your stead. And suppose that that good man not only thus gained your freedom by giving up his own dear son, but also got a beautiful kingdom for you. Would not you believe that this person loved and cared for you more than any one else in the world?

Now, your heavenly FATHER *has* given you this greatest proof of His love that could be given. You have, no doubt, often disobeyed Him and grieved Him by wicked tempers, or untruthfulness, or disobedience. And you deserved to have been left in the power of the Evil One, your cruel enemy, who would have kept you in never-ending slavery, and tormented you more dreadfully than you can think. But GOD your FATHER gave His only SON, Who took upon Him the form of a slave, and suffered cruel ill-treatment, and died on the cross to set you free from the power of the devil, and to win for you a glorious kingdom. "GOD commendeth His love toward us, in that, while we were yet sinners, CHRIST died for us." Can you not trust His love after such a proof of it as this, and believe that whatever He tells you to do or not to do it is best for your happiness to obey? And will you not obey Him just because He loves you so? A little boy was once tempted to steal some apples from an orchard. His companions said to him, "You may safely do it, your father is so fond of you that he will not beat you if you are found out." "No, no," said the little fellow, "that is the very reason why I would not do it; for I should grieve my father who is so kind and good to me."

Now let us think awhile of that kingdom which it is your kind FATHER's good pleasure to give you.

You know that it is a great thing to have a kingdom; but it is not every one who is fit to be trusted with a kingdom. Your History of England will tell you that, and you will have learnt there what mischief has been done by bad and foolish kings. To be a good king one must first learn the rules of the kingdom; and to rule others we must first learn to obey. So you must first learn to be good subjects, and to respect and obey the laws of GOD's kingdom on earth before you can be safely entrusted with a kingdom in heaven. Now, GOD's kingdom on earth is His Church. So you must first be faithful and true members of His Church, and obey its rules and submit yourselves to all your governors, teachers, spiritual pastors and masters. The Church is GOD's kingdom on earth, in which you may be trained so as to be fit for His kingdom in heaven. But who may paint the glories of that kingdom? "Eye hath not seen, nor ear heard, neither have entered into the heart of man the things

which GOD hath prepared for them that love Him."
This Church of JESUS, His kingdom on earth, will be
purified from all sin and imperfection, "all things that
offend" will be cast out of it. He will "present it to
Himself a glorious Church, not having spot or wrinkle
or any such thing, but holy and without blemish." All
its members will be good and pure, and holy; all will
live together in perfect love and happiness. All will
see JESUS in His glory, the King in His beauty, and
they who have suffered with Him will also reign with
Him; they who have overcome will sit down with
Him in His throne, even as He overcame and is set
down with His FATHER in His throne. Oh, dear
children, to think that you and I should have this
hope set before us of sharing with JESUS the un-
speakable glories of His kingdom! How awful the
loss if we should miss it by our own folly and wickedness! How blessed to win it! And we may all win
it, if we will; for JESUS has won it for us, and we have
only to believe it, and learn to love Him, and to be
good, obedient and true members of His kingdom on
earth, faithful and true to JESUS amid the trials and
temptations of this life, and our FATHER will give us
this beautiful kingdom, and make us kings and priests
in it to be before His throne and to serve Him day
and night in His temple. Will you not, then, "seek
first the kingdom of GOD and His righteousness," re-
membering His promise, "they that seek, find," and
while on earth try to live heavenly lives, to think holy
and heavenly thoughts, and to prepare yourselves by
GOD's grace for that place which JESUS has gone to
prepare for you?

III.

LOOKING UNTO JESUS.

"Looking unto Jesus."—Heb. xii. 2.

My dear children, did you ever see men running a race ? If so you will have noticed that a great crowd of people were looking on, that the runners had stripped themselves of all that would hinder their swiftness, and that their faces were all turned in the direction of the winning-post, their eyes eagerly fixed on the end or goal to which they were hastening. Well, the writer of this Epistle to the Hebrews had evidently seen such a race, and he says that the life of Christians must be something like it. He tells us that *we* have got a race to run, and that there are a great many spectators, holy men and women and children who have run their race, and whose spirits are resting in Paradise, but who are watching with great interest us who are still running. We too, if we would win that race and safely reach the goal, must strip ourselves of everything that would hinder our journey to heaven. We must lay aside every weight, every clog and hindrance, and the sin which does so easily beset us—bad tempers, greediness, lying, and such like. I will tell you a story which illustrates this. There was once a captain of a band of robbers named Akaba. He had great heaps of treasures in his cave which he had stolen. But, though he was so rich, he was not happy. His mind was ill at ease. So he went to a dervish famous for his goodness, living on the borders of a wilderness in Arabia, and thus addressed him: "Five hundred swords obey my nod, innumerable slaves bow to my control, my storehouses are filled with silver and gold; tell me how can I add to all these the hope of eternal life?" The dervish led him to a rugged mountain track, pointed to three immense stones, and told him to take them and follow him to the top of the hill. Akaba took them up, but with such a weight he could scarcely move. One by one he was obliged to leave them, and then easily climbed the hill. "My son," said the hermit, when they had sat on the top, "you have a threefold burden to hinder you on the road to a better state. Dismiss the robber band, set your slaves free, give back your ill-gotten gain. Sooner would Akaba reach the mountain-top, bearing those heavy stones, than gain eternal life encumbered by power, lust, and wealth." And it is said that Akaba obeyed the dervish. We must "go and do likewise," put away all sinful habits and evil ways, and press on our heavenward way. And more than this, we must have our faces in the right direction. Men cannot run well if they keep looking behind them and on every side—they must look straight before them. And it is written that we are to run "looking unto JESUS." JESUS is our goal. To run to Him is to run to heaven; to look to Him is to look to heaven. For where JESUS is *there* is heaven. Children, all your life through you must look to JESUS. True, you cannot see Him yet with your eyes, but you can keep Him always in your mind, like David, who said, "I have set the LORD always before me." Look

to Him for salvation, look to Him as your example,
look to Him for help. Let nothing make you turn
away your eyes, the eyes of your soul, from Him.
Pray that you may be able to do this.

> " O may no earthborn cloud arise
> To hide Thee from Thy servant's eyes."

Look nowhere else for salvation ; set no other example
before you ; lift your eyes nowhere else for help.

You remember how the Israelites had sinned against
GOD, and GOD punished them by sending fiery serpents among them which bit them so that many of
them died. And when the people confessed their
sins, and Moses prayed for them, GOD told Moses
to make a serpent of brass and to set it upon a pole,
that every one who was bitten, if he looked upon it
might live. Now, JESUS CHRIST said that every one
must look to Him, that is, believe in Him, as the
Israelites looked to the brazen serpent, believing that
so they would be saved from the serpent's bite. .He
said to Nicodemus, " As Moses lifted up the serpent
in the wilderness, even so must the Son of Man be
lifted up ; that whosoever believeth in Him should
not perish, but have eternal life." So, to look to
JESUS for salvation, means to believe in Him, to trust
in Him and in Him only for salvation. Only it must
not be a mere passing look. We must not look once
and then turn away. No, we must look, and look,
and look again, fill our minds with that wonderful
sight, JESUS lifted up upon the Cross, until there is no
room left in our hearts for any other love but the love
of JESUS, no other sight which so fills our minds and

touches our hearts, and draws out all the trust and affection that is in them, as the sight of JESUS dying for sinners on the cross. The saints of old who lived and died before CHRIST came were saved by such looking as this. They did not indeed receive the promises of His coming, but they died in faith, "having seen them afar off, and were persuaded of them and embraced them." And all who have been saved since have been saved in the same way—they looked to JESUS only, and lived and died trusting their all to Him.

Then, children, you must look to JESUS as your example to copy. You know when you are learning to write you look at the copy which is set you, and if you would write well and keep from mistakes, you must keep looking at your copy. If you look only once at your copy when you are writing the first line, and afterwards look at your own line which you have just written, you will not write well. If you make a mistake in any line you will keep on making it in every line that follows, and each line will get less like the copy. So you must keep looking to the example of JESUS, or you will make sad mistakes in your life, and keep repeating them until your life will become a very bad copy at last of that which JESUS has set you. JESUS is a pattern for every child of obedience to parents. We read in the holy Gospel how that He went down to Nazareth and was subject unto Mary and Joseph—that is, He minded what they said to Him, and did as they bade Him. He is a pattern to every child of teachableness and willingness to learn, for He was found in the Temple, sitting at the feet of the teachers of the law of GOD, listening attentively to them and asking them questions.   And so, too, in His gentleness and kindness, and truthfulness, and love of prayer and of the house of GOD, little children as well as grown-up people can see a perfect copy for them to follow.

But no one can copy that perfect example without help.   And for help, too, you must look to JESUS. He will help you if you do but ask Him.   He does not tell you to do things, show you how to live, and then leave you in your helplessness to set about them. He is not a hard Master, like Pharaoh, who told the people to make bricks and would not give them straw, but left them to find straw for themselves as best they might.   When He told the man with the withered hand to stretch it out, He gave him the power to do it.   And so you may be quite sure, that if you look to Him, and pray to Him to help you to trust Him and love Him, and copy Him, He will do so.   He will help you by giving you His HOLY SPIRIT.   Just as certainly as if a child asks its father or mother for food they would not give their child a stone, so certainly and much more certainly will your FATHER in heaven give the HOLY SPIRIT to them that ask Him.   For JESUS has said so.

Let these words, then, dear children, be the motto of your lives, " Looking unto JESUS."   When you are tempted to do wrong think of JESUS, and look to Him for help.   If you have sinned, whatever be the fault, look to JESUS.   Think of Him nailed to the cross, and saying, " See, My child, what I suffered for you; what it cost Me to get that sin of yours forgiven.   Go,

My child, you are forgiven; but go, and sin no more."

When you are in doubt whether you may do a thing or no, or what it is your duty to do, look to JESUS, and think, "What would He have done? What would it please Him to see me do?" Don't look at your companions to see what they think right or wrong; don't copy any one, or try to please any one but JESUS only, and then you will, like Him, increase "in wisdom and in stature, and in favour with GOD and man."

IV.

TEMPLES OF THE HOLY GHOST.

" What? Know ye not that your body is a temple of the Holy Ghost Which is in you, Which ye have of God, and ye are not your own?"—1 Cor. vi. 19.

FIRST of all, Christian children, I must say a few words to you about GOD, that I may be sure that you know who the HOLY GHOST is, Whose temple or church your bodies are. You have, no doubt, been taught that there is only one GOD—that, although the FATHER is GOD, and JESUS is GOD, and the HOLY GHOST is GOD, yet these three are but one GOD, not three GODS. You cannot understand *how* this can be, nor can I, nor any man ; but we know for certain that it is true. The FATHER, the SON, and the HOLY GHOST are not merely different names for the same Being. The FATHER is not the SON, and neither of

c

them is the HOLY GHOST. Each is a distinct Person,
but each has the same nature of GOD. So the HOLY
GHOST is GOD. We sometimes call Him the HOLY
SPIRIT, because a ghost is the same as a spirit. If
you had no bodies you would be ghosts or spirits. To
die is to "give up the ghost,"—that is, the ghost leaves
the body and then the body is dead. There are many
spirits. Angels are spirits. Good angels are good
spirits, wicked angels, or devils, are evil spirits. *We*
are spirits, but spirits living in bodies. GOD is a
Spirit. He is called in the Epistle to the Hebrews,
"the FATHER of spirits." He made all those spirits
which we call angels, and He made *us* spirit, soul, and
body. He is *the* Spirit; FATHER, SON, and HOLY
GHOST, all three are one GOD, Who is a Spirit. And
we call the Third Person of this Blessed Trinity "the
HOLY SPIRIT." We cannot *see* a spirit with our bodily
eyes, we cannot see the angels any more than we can
see wind or air, much less can we see GOD. "No man
hath seen GOD at any time." For us to see a spirit, it
must take some form, as angels have been permitted to
do sometimes that they might appear to men. Men
have seen JESUS CHRIST Who is GOD; but they only
saw His human body when He was made man; they
did not see His Godhead, although He was GOD all
the time as well as man, as He is now, and ever will
be. No man has seen the HOLY GHOST. He was
seen once in the form of a dove settling upon JESUS
CHRIST at His Baptism. But what was seen was only
the dove's form or appearance, not the HOLY GHOST
Himself. Again, when the HOLY GHOST came down
upon the disciples on the day of Pentecost, there

appeared to them flames of fire like tongues divided, which rested upon each of them, without however burning them or scorching them at all; but these were only outward signs to show that the HOLY GHOST had come upon them, as JESUS had promised that He should; *they* were not the HOLY GHOST. He was not seen. The HOLY GHOST does not show now by any outward appearance either of a dove or flames of fire that He rests upon any one or dwells in him; but He makes His presence *felt*. You cannot see the wind, but you can feel it and see its effects. So those in whom the HOLY GHOST dwells feel that He is in them, and show that He is in them by the sort of lives they lead. They feel that He is in them when they feel something which gives them the wish and the power to be good and to do right, which makes them afraid and unwilling to do wrong, and makes them feel unhappy and ashamed if they *have* done wrong. These are ways in which His Presence is *felt*. And when people are seen to be living Christian lives, and to be kind and gentle and forgiving, patient, humble, truthful and obedient, and so on, these are signs which show that the HOLY GHOST is working in them.

Now I want you to remember always that your *bodies* are the HOLY GHOST's temples. Did you ever see a Church consecrated? Well, at any rate you know that every Church has been consecrated—that is, solemnly set apart for the worship of GOD as a holy place. Now, when you were brought to the Font, and were baptized, as you sometimes see babies brought now, you were consecrated, your bodies were set apart to be holy, temples for GOD the HOLY GHOST to dwell

in.   Every part of a Church is holy—the porch, the
tower, the nave or body of the Church, the aisles or
side parts, and the chancel, or part where the Altar or
holy Table stands.   Everything in it is holy to the
LORD, the Font, the Altar, the choir stalls, the pulpit,
the organ, the bells, all were solemnly set apart for
the sacred service of GOD, and separated from all
common uses.   So every part of your bodies is holy to
the LORD, as parts of His holy Temple; your eyes, your
ears, your tongue, your hands, all were consecrated to
His service, and must not be used for any sinful purposes.   They are not your own to use as you like ;
they are GOD'S, and you must use them in His service.
You know it would be very shocking to use the Font
as a common wash-hand-basin, or the LORD's Table for
common meals, or any part of the Church as a play-
room or drawing-room, or the organ or harmonium to
play common tunes on, or to ring the bells just for
amusement.   But it is *much more shocking* and wicked
for a baptized Christian to use his ears to listen to
sinful words, his tongue to tell lies or say what is
wicked, his eyes to look at improper objects or to
read bad books, his mouth to eat and drink greedily,
or his hands to pick and steal, or to use any part of
his body in an immodest or impure or sinful way.
For to do such things is to defile by sin the temple of
the HOLY GHOST, and to make Him very grieved and
angry.   S. Paul says, " If any man defile the temple
of GOD, him shall GOD destroy ; for the temple of GOD
is holy, which temple ye are."   If Christians use the
members of their bodies for sinful purposes, they grieve
the HOLY SPIRIT of GOD, and at last, if they do not

repent, He leaves them and will not dwell any longer in a place so defiled by sin. So S. Paul writes, *" Quench not the Spirit."* But we must not only *not* use a Church or any part of it for a *wrong* purpose ; we must use it for a *right* purpose—that is, as a House of prayer and praise. Would it not be a sad sight to see a disused Church ?—a Church shut up and never used for the service of GOD all the year round ? Yes, surely it would be, and *I* think that it is a sad sight to see a Church only opened on *Sundays* and not *every* day. Well, so it is with the bodies of Christians. It is very sad when baptized Christians pass day after day without prayer, and Sunday after Sunday without going to Church ! It is like a shut up, unused Church, *only sadder*, for *these* are *living* temples in which is never, or seldom heard, the voice of prayer and praise. A prayerless Christian is a silent, useless house of GOD left to fall into decay and ruin.

Oh, dear children, let your bodies be like carefully kept, frequently used Churches, never profaned by aught that is sinful or unclean, from which the praises of GOD and the voice of earnest prayer regularly ascend to His throne above ; let your hearts be as Altars, ever keeping alive the remembrance of the sacrifice of the death of CHRIST, your consciences as preachers in the pulpit, ever warning you to avoid evil and to follow that which is good, your tongues like the organ and the sweet bells sounding the praises of GOD, all your senses and all your powers employed in His service, so that " whether you eat or drink, or whatsoever you do, you may do all to the glory of GOD." Do not be like shut up Churches, do not be like Churches opened only on

Sundays, as if religion were only for one day in the week. Be like Churches open every day, morning and evening. Every day lift up your hearts with your voices in prayer and praise, and let your commonest actions, words, and thoughts, of every day of the week be hallowed by the remembrance that you act, and speak, and think, as temples of GOD the HOLY GHOST. Pray to that Blessed SPIRIT Himself to will and to do in you of His good pleasure ; never disobey His voice speaking to your heart. Never do or say what He makes you feel is wrong ; always when He puts into your heart a wish to do anything right and good and kind, be sure you do it ; and reverence your bodies as His sacred temples, never polluting any part of them by making it a minister of sin. So, keeping your-selves, by His grace, pure and unspotted from the world, you shall form part of that glorious Church, holy and without blemish, which JESUS shall present to Himself at the last, which is builded together for an habitation of GOD through the SPIRIT, and which through all eternity shall be illuminated by the in-dwelling Presence of the LORD GOD Almighty and the LAMB, and whereinto shall enter nothing that defileth.

V.

THE CATHOLIC CHURCH.

"And the Lord added to the Church daily such as should be saved."—Acts ii. 47.

MY dear children, you have learned to say in the Creed, "I believe in the Holy Catholic Church." Did you ever think what these words mean? It is very important that you should know. I will try, therefore, to make it as clear and as interesting to you as I can. The word "Church" is commonly used in two senses; sometimes it means all baptized Christians, sometimes it means the building in which Christians meet to worship GOD. In the Creed it means, not the building, but the whole body of Christian people who are baptized, and hold the Catholic Faith, i.e. the Faith or Belief set forth in the creeds. The word "Catholic" means "universal;" and the Church is called Catholic because it is not made up of people from one nation only, as the Jewish Church; but people of all nations may, and do, belong to it. It is also called "Catholic" because it teaches the true faith which it has always taught, and which it received by revelation from GOD. There is only one Catholic Church in all the world. There cannot be more. JESUS CHRIST did not come to found a number of different churches. But as there is *one* LORD, *one* Spirit, *one* Faith, *one* Baptism, so also there is *one* Body, that is one Church which is called the Body of CHRIST, i.e., a body of people joined to CHRIST, and made one with Him and with each other in Holy Baptism. But as a body has many different parts, so there are different parts of the Catholic Church. One part is the Roman Catholic Church; another, the Greek, or Eastern Church; another is our own English Church, which is the Catholic Church in England. These are, as it were, main trunks or limbs of the body, CHRIST being the Head of all, as your body has legs and arms. But each main part of your body is made up of small portions, and so the whole Church and each part of it is made up of individual Christians, but all together make one Catholic Church.

Then, a great many members of this Catholic Church are no longer living upon earth; but they are still members of the same Catholic Church, they have not ceased to belong to it because they are dead (that is, if they lived and died as faithful Christians should), they have only passed out of our sight to wait in Paradise until CHRIST shall come to raise up their bodies again, and to present the Catholic Church to Himself, "a glorious Church without spot or wrinkle or any such thing, but holy and without blemish."

Very well, then, "I believe in the Holy Catholic Church" means, as it always has meant, a belief in the Church which JESUS CHRIST founded, and which the HOLY GHOST dwells in as a soul dwells in a body, that same Church of which the text says that "the LORD added to it daily such as should be saved," that same Church which, beginning like a grain of mustard-seed for smallness, has grown and extended, and struck its roots deep into the soil, and spread out its branches into all lands, a branch of which overshadows this our

land of England. The *same* Church, although here
and there disfigured and maimed, although not every-
where in all things alike, having some branches lopped
off, some unfruitful, some bearing corrupt fruit, just as
an old churchyard yew-tree is the same tree that grew
there hundreds of years ago, although age and many
storms have passed over it since then and so changed
its appearance, that our forefathers, who lived when it
was a young sapling, would not be able to know it for
the same tree. Like that old yew-tree, too, the Church
has struck its roots deeper and deeper into the soil.
Marred and rent and disfigured in those parts which
are above the earth and seen by the eyes of men,
there lie below the ground, out of sight, vast roots
resting quietly, safe from storm and tempest, even the
faithful departed members of CHRIST's Church waiting
in the rest of Paradise for the final triumph and glory
of the whole.

The Holy Catholic Church began on the day of
Pentecost—(the Christian name of which day is Whit-
sun-day), when the HOLY GHOST came down upon a
small body of faithful disciples of the LORD JESUS,
and to that infant Church the LORD added in that day
three thousand souls; from that day the LORD kept
adding to the number more and more, Jews and Gentiles, people of all nations and kindreds and tongues,
till it numbered members in all parts of the world, in
Europe, in Asia, in Africa, in America, and Australia ;
it is all one Church, having one Head, one LORD,
one Faith, one Baptism, one GOD and FATHER of all,
one HOLY SPIRIT guiding, blessing, and sanctifying in
every part of the whole Body—all is built on that one

Foundation, which is JESUS CHRIST. The HOLY GHOST dwells in it, as a soul in a body, giving it spiritual life, giving power to the preaching of its ministers, to the Sacraments administered by its priests, and grace to all its members. All the members of this great society, the Catholic Church, *may* be saved if they will. The Sacraments, the preaching of the Word, and other means of grace, are freely offered to all. Those who use them rightly will be saved; those who neglect or misuse them will be lost.

Take care, dear children, that you do not mistake the meaning of the text. Our English Bible is, you know, translated out of the languages in which it was written into our own tongue. And, as a whole, this has been wonderfully well done; but this passage is not quite correctly translated. It does not mean, as it almost seems to mean, that all would be certainly saved who were added to the Church. It means that the LORD added to the Church such as were being saved—that is, that all who were added to the Church were placed in a state of salvation, in a state in which as long as they continued they would be safe. GOD saved all the children of Israel from the bondage of the Egyptians. He overthrew their enemies in the Red Sea, and led *them* safely through it, and placed them in the wilderness, free to go on to the promised land, and if they had all gone on, and had had faith in GOD and obeyed Him, they would all have got safely over Jordan into the land of Promise ; but we know that with many of them GOD was not well pleased. They rebelled against Him, and would not trust in Him, and so most of them were " overthrown

in the wilderness," and never got to that good land
which GOD had promised to give them. So, in the
Catholic Church all have passed through the waters of
Baptism, and been delivered from the guilt and bondage of original sin, and placed in a state of freedom
and safety; but many, alas! do not continue in that
state. They fall away into sin and unbelief, and lose
the promised land of Heaven. For when we call the
Catholic Church "holy," we do not mean that all her
members are holy and good. Would that they were!
But no, as in one of our LORD'S parables, the wheat
and the tares were to grow together until the harvest,
as in another He likened the kingdom of Heaven,
that is, the Church, to a net cast into the sea, which
gathered in both bad fishes and good, so in His
Church, good and bad, holy and worthless people are
mixed together until the LORD JESUS CHRIST comes
to separate them and to cast out of His kingdom all
things that offend. Still, the Church is holy, because
CHRIST, her Head, is holy, and because all her members are dedicated to GOD, and she possesses the
means of making men truly holy through the Word of
GOD and the Sacraments, and, though all her members
are not holy, yet the Spirit which dwells in her is the
HOLY GHOST. And, one day, this Church of JESUS
will be holy in all her members. When that bright
day comes there will no longer be any error, or divi-
sion, or imperfection in her. There will be no im-
purity, no spot or stain of sin found in her. There
will be no pain, or sorrow, or poverty, or suffering, or
death seen in any of her members, because there will
be no sin which causes all these evils. And every heart

will be full of the love of JESUS, and every eye will
flash with joy, and every tongue sing songs of praise,
and every pulse beat high with rapture, because JESUS
is there in the midst of His Church, seen in all the
beauty and glory of His unveiled Presence.

I believe in that holy Catholic Church, holy in all
her members, Catholic in that she will embrace in her
bosom people of all nations and kindred and tongues.
I believe in her future glory and triumph and perfect
happiness.   I believe that this will be the same Church
which JESUS filled with His Holy Spirit at Pentecost,
to which He added daily such as were being saved.
And what I believe, you, my dear children, believe
too, do you not?   And if we do believe this of the
Holy Catholic Church, oh, let us use diligence to
make our calling and election sure, that we may continue in this holy Church to all eternity, and not be
cast out of her when all things that offend and defile
shall be cast out.   May the LORD Who added you to
His Church in Holy Baptism keep you in this state of
salvation to your life's end !

VI.

THE NEW BIRTH.

*" Jesus answered, Verily, verily, I say unto thee, Except a man
be born of water and of the Spirit, he cannot enter into the kingdom
of God."*—S. John iii. 5.

OUR LORD JESUS CHRIST had been doing so many
miracles at Jerusalem, that some of the people began

to believe that He really must be the CHRIST Who
was to come, and among others, one of the rulers,
Nicodemus by name. But, as none of the other
rulers believed in Him, and as they were very angry
with any one who did, Nicodemus was afraid to say
openly what he thought, and, although he wanted
very much to know more of this wonderful Teacher,
he did not dare to be seen speaking to Him. So he
came to JESUS by night, and said, "Rabbi, we know
that Thou art a Teacher come from GOD ; for no man
can do these miracles that Thou doest, except GOD
be with him." Now you may perhaps think it was
very cowardly of Nicodemus to come and make this
confession of his faith in JESUS as a "Teacher come
from GOD," by night and in secret. And, no doubt,
it would have been much braver had he come and
said it openly before all men and in the light of day.
But we must remember that Nicodemus was as yet
only an inquirer, and not a full believer in JESUS
CHRIST. It requires a very real belief in JESUS to
confess Him boldly before people who do not believe
in Him, and who would laugh at us and illuse us for
doing so. And it was no small thing in those times
for any one to believe in JESUS at all when every one
else was against Him. So Nicodemus came, timidly, it
is true, but still he came, and expressed himself willing
to be taught by JESUS. And JESUS began by teaching
something that sounded very strange indeed to him.
He told him that he could not even see the kingdom of
GOD unless he was born again. No doubt Nicodemus
had come to hear all about the kingdom which CHRIST
was going to set up, thinking it was an earthly king-

dom, and that He was going to make the Jewish
nation the greatest of all nations, and to make it more
glorious than it had been in the days of King Solomon.
So he must have been very much astonished to be
told that no one could so much as see the kingdom
which JESUS had come to establish unless he were
born afresh. But what JESUS meant was that His
kingdom was not of this world. It was a spiritual
kingdom, the kingdom of GOD, and that it required
faith to see it, and that a man's nature must become
changed and made new by the Spirit of GOD, that he
might have faith to believe in that kingdom. So
S. Paul wrote to the Corinthians, "The natural man
receiveth not the things of the Spirit of GOD : for they
are foolishness unto him ; neither can he know them,
because they are spiritually discerned." Well, Nicodemus did not understand all this. He took our
LORD's words in their plain, natural meaning, and
asked, "How can a man be born when he is old ?"
But he might have known that our LORD was speaking
of a change to be brought about in him by means of
Baptism, for Nicodemus was a "master of Israel," and
knew quite well that when Jews baptized Gentiles,
that is, people of other nations, who believed in the
true GOD, they used to call them "infants just born."
So our LORD goes on to refer more plainly to Baptism
as the means of the new birth. "Verily, verily, I say
unto thee, Except a man be born of water and of the
Spirit, he cannot enter into the kingdom of GOD ;" and
then He explained to Nicodemus that He had been
sent into the world by the FATHER to be the SAVIOUR
of all who would believe in Him, and that He must be

"lifted up," that is, crucified on the cross, as Moses lifted up the serpent in the wilderness on a pole, and that, as the people were saved from the fiery serpents by looking on that brazen one, so whoever looked to JESUS for salvation would be saved.

But we will not think any more now about Nicodemus; I want you to think about Baptism and the new birth. Our LORD said that every one must be born afresh by a new and spiritual birth before they can enter into the kingdom of GOD, that is, His Church; and that the outward means and sign of this new birth is the water of Baptism. And before His ascension into Heaven He told His Apostles to go and make disciples or Christians of all nations, "baptizing them into the Name of the FATHER, and of the SON, and of the HOLY GHOST." And so the Catechism teaches you that the outward visible sign or form in Baptism is "water; wherein the person is baptized in the Name of the FATHER, and of the SON, and of the HOLY GHOST," and that the inward and spiritual grace is "a death unto sin and a new birth unto righteousness:" and then it goes on to give you the reason why this new birth is needed—because we are "by nature born in sin, and the children of wrath."

Now I know that it is very difficult for you to understand how it is that every child that is born into the world is a sinner, and, innocent as it looks, is a child of wrath. But listen, and I will try to make it as plain as I can. GOD made Adam and Eve, the first man and woman, innocent and good, without any evil nature inclining them to sin; but the devil tempted Eve to disobey GOD, and she was persuaded by him and sinned, and then she in her turn persuaded Adam, and he sinned too. From that time their nature was changed; as if they were born again they became different creatures, and were now of their own nature inclined to sin. And they could not help handing down this evil nature to their children and their children's children. So every child is by nature born in sin, it belongs to a race of beings who have become sinful, it needs to have that sin which it inherits from its parents forgiven; and it needs to have a new nature given to it which may get the better of the evil nature. That sin, stained with which each child is born into the world, can only be cleansed away by the precious Blood of CHRIST, and that new nature can only be given by the HOLY SPIRIT. This is done in Baptism. So we say in the Creed which is repeated at Holy Communion, "I acknowledge one Baptism for the remission of sins," that is, "for the forgiveness of sins." When you were baptized for the sake of JESUS CHRIST Who died for you, that sin with which you were born into the world was forgiven you, and also, for the sake of CHRIST, a new power, called "grace," was given to you by the HOLY SPIRIT, by which you may overcome your sinful nature if you choose, and you were made a child of GOD in CHRIST JESUS.

Perhaps it will make all this plainer if you think how many different kinds of animals there are, and remember that each kind is born with a nature of its own. For instance, it is the nature of adders to bite. If you found a brood of young adders, you would not wait till they were older to see if they would bite. You would know that they would be sure to do so, because it is their nature, it is *in* them. So you would kill them all, although they were quite innocent of having ever done any harm, because you know that from their very nature they would become dangerous and mischievous if they grew up. Well, in the same way, GOD sees sin in the very nature of a little child just born. It has not yet done anything wrong, but GOD sees that it is its nature to do so by-and-by unless it is either killed and not allowed to grow up, or has a new and better nature given to it which may master the old one. So GOD in His mercy and love forgives the child its sinful nature, the sin that is in it, and gives it by His Holy Spirit a new and better nature, and He has appointed Holy Baptism as a means of conveying to the child these blessings, and a sign or pledge to assure it that it has received them.

GOD *might* have destroyed all the human race, just as you might destroy a brood of poisonous serpents. It would not have been cruel. It would only have been strict justice. But, for the sake of His dear SON, JESUS CHRIST, He has mercy upon us, forgives us our sins, and gives us His grace, that we may keep from fresh sins, and be able to love Him and believe in Him, and so come at last to His kingdom in Heaven, His purified and glorious Church. Then, since GOD has been so good and gracious to you, dear children, see that you do not let that evil nature get the upper hand ; but fight against it in the power of the grace which GOD has given to you, and which He is ever ready to give you more and more, as you need it, if you " call for" it " by diligent prayer." You must feel that you have something in you which inclines you to choose evil rather than good, and another something which makes you wish and try to do what is right. That which inclines you to evil is your fallen, sinful nature; the other and better feeling comes from the new nature, the grace of GOD the HOLY SPIRIT. You have power to choose which shall get the better and be the master over the other. Oh, what a struggle it is sometimes! How sad when the sinful nature wins the battle! how joyful when grace triumphs, and the evil is resisted! How happy you feel! how angry the devil is, beaten by a little child! how the angels rejoice! How JESUS smiles upon you! GOD grant you many such victories for His dear SON'S sake, and give you strength to persevere to the end, so that, being faithful unto death, He may give you the crown of life!

VII.

PREPARE TO MEET THY GOD.

for Advent.

" Prepare to meet thy God."—Amos iv. 12.

ADVENT! What does that word mean? No doubt, children, you could tell me. It means " coming," does it not? Yes; and Who is coming? JESUS CHRIST is coming. He came once; He will come again. He came once as a little baby; He will come again in power and great glory. When will He come?

We do not know. Perhaps to-day, perhaps to-morrow, perhaps in a week or so, perhaps not for years. We do not know. He has not told us. Nobody knows. But He will certainly come, and we shall see Him. He has told us that. What will He do when He comes? You know; He will come to judge us all. All who are alive now and who ever lived, small and great, will stand before Him to be judged. What does that mean? Does it mean to punish us all? No, to punish some, to reward others; you know that everybody is not punished who is brought before an earthly judge. Some people are falsely accused of crimes which they never committed. They are brought before a judge and a jury of twelve men. The judge and jury are told what the person is accused of having done. He is asked if he is guilty of having done it, or not guilty. Then witnesses are called, some for the prisoner, some against him. Lawyers speak, some for the prisoner, some against him. The judge and jury listen carefully to what is said on both sides, and then the jury say whether they think the man guilty or not guilty, and the judge gives sentence accordingly. If the person is found guilty, the judge says how he is to be punished. If he is found not guilty, the judge orders him to be let go free. But in all earthly judgments there *may* be mistakes. Some witnesses may tell lies, and an innocent person may be punished or a guilty one escape. Then, again, when a person is found not guilty, the judge does not give him any reward. But when JESUS CHRIST comes to judge all men, no mistakes will be possible, because JESUS CHRIST is GOD, and

He knows the thoughts of all men, so if witnesses tell
lies, they will not be able to deceive Him. And
again, JESUS CHRIST is different from all earthly judges
in this, that He will give rewards to all who are not
found to deserve punishment. In that judgment the
devil will accuse us all. The witnesses will be our
consciences, the people to whom we have done good
or evil, evil spirits who have tempted us, our guardian
angels who have watched over us. Some will bear
witness in our favour, some will bear witness against
us. The devil will be the lawyer who will demand
our punishment. Who will be our Advocate, the
Lawyer to speak for us and demand our acquittal?
Why, the Judge Himself, JESUS CHRIST, if we take
Him now, trust in Him now, as our SAVIOUR. Then
we shall be sure to be acquitted — that is, pro-
nounced "not guilty." And if so, the Judge will
reward us. Not that we deserve it ; it will be His
free gift. And what a reward it will be !—eternal life
with JESUS and all His holy saints and angels in
heaven. But what if JESUS cannot say a word for us ?
What if the devil brings true witnesses to prove that
we never loved JESUS, never tried to serve Him and
keep His commandments ; that to the last we loved
sin and went our own wilful way, and never sought
pardon for our sins and grace to do better? What if
the Evil One proves that we lived and died without
CHRIST, and shut our hearts against Him who died to
save us ? What then ? Why, the devil will say,
" This person would not have your mercy ; I claim
him of your justice." And there will be nothing to
be said against his claim. The Judge who wanted to

show mercy, but you would not let Him, must now deal with you in strict justice. He cannot be unjust even to a devil. The devil must have his own, and the terrible sentence must go forth from the lips of the Judge, " Depart from Me, ye cursed, into everlasting fire prepared for the devil and his angels."

Do you believe this, children ? Then surely you must live as those who believe that they will certainly be judged. Surely you must " Prepare to meet your GOD." If any one is accused of a crime, and is going to be tried for his life, what does he do ? Why, he gets all the witnesses he can to speak for him. He secures the ablest and cleverest advocate to plead his cause. He makes every preparation he can to meet his judge. Well, we, you and I, are going to be accused, are going to be tried before JESUS as our Judge ; our eternal life or death hangs upon the sentence which He will then give. Shall we not prepare ? The devil, our accuser, is even now preparing his witnesses against us. He will bring against us all that we have thought or said or done wrong, all that we have left undone that we ought to have done. Shall we not prepare ? Shall we not get ready our witnesses to speak for us ? Shall we not take care to have the LORD JESUS as our Advocate, our SAVIOUR ? How can you prepare, my children ? What can you do ? First, you can keep getting rid of every witness that Satan wants to bring against you. And you can do this by getting your sins forgiven now. Then, if Satan brings them up against you in that day, the Judge will not receive them as witnesses against you. He will say, It is true the child committed these sins, but they were pardoned, blotted out long ago; you cannot use them as evidence. Remember this, dear children, sins which you repent of and confess to JESUS and ask GOD to forgive for JESUS' sake, can never be brought up against you. Then, you can be getting witnesses to speak for you. You can be dutiful, obedient, and truthful to your parents, clergy, and teachers, and try to save them trouble; then they will be witnesses for you. You can do acts of kindness and love to your brothers and sisters, schoolfellows and playmates, to the sick and needy, and then they will be witnesses for you. You can give money to help to send missionaries to the heathen instead of spending all on toys or sweets, and then missionaries and those to whom they are sent will be witnesses for you. Every one whom you help and show kindness to, yes, even poor dumb animals which you treat kindly, instead of cruelly teasing and tormenting them, will be witnesses for you. So you see you can keep taking the devil's witnesses from him, and you can keep getting more and more witnesses to speak for you. And in doing thus, because you believe in JESUS and love Him, and do good to all men and animals because JESUS made and loves and cares for them, you will be securing JESUS as your Advocate to speak for you. If He sees you sorry when you sin, because you have grieved Him, and caring for those for whom He cares because you want to please Him, then He is on your side. He will say in that day, Your sins are all blotted out and shall be remembered no more against you. You were heartily sorry and asked My forgiveness, so you are forgiven. I bore their punishment for you, so you are free. And inasmuch as you did acts of kindness and love to others, you did them to Me. Come, ye blessed children of My FATHER receive the kingdom prepared for you from the beginning of the world. Will it not be joyful to hear such words as these?

So you see that you can "prepare to meet your GOD." And if you are so preparing to meet Him, His second coming to judge the world need not, ought not to be a thought of terror to you. No, rather, dear children, if your sins are blotted out for His Name's sake, and you are trying to love Him and please Him, you will look forward to that day with joy. You will mean what you say when you pray, "Thy kingdom come," for the coming of GOD's kingdom will be the coming of your kingdom too, that kingdom of which you were made inheritors at your baptism. You will be able to say, "Even so, come quickly, LORD JESUS," —for you will feel that He is coming for *you*, coming to fetch you away to be with Him, coming to take you where there will be no more pain, nor sorrow, nor want, nor sin, where your little eyes will never be wet with tears, your hands and feet never pinched with cold, where you will ever be laughing joyously and singing sweetly, and playing happily and employed usefully, where you will see beautiful sights and beautiful people, and JESUS Himself the most lovely of all ; where you will hear beautiful sounds and voices, and the voice of JESUS the sweetest of all, and, yourselves lovely and innocent, without one sinful thought or wish, you will be able to fly more swiftly than the birds from star to star, admiring all the glories and wonders of

that beautiful kingdom which the love of JESUS has
prepared for your everlasting home.

You won't, dear children, will you, risk the loss of
all this for want of preparing to meet your GOD?

VIII.

CHRIST COMING AS THE DEW.

For Christmas Day.

*" He shall come down like the rain into a fleece of wool, even as
the drops that water the earth."*—Psalm lxxii. 6.

"THIS day is this Scripture fulfilled in your ears."
For it is a prophecy of the coming of our LORD JESUS
CHRIST. No doubt the Psalmist had in his mind the
sign of Gideon's fleece. You remember that GOD told
Gideon that He would save Israel from their enemies,
the Midianites, by Gideon's hand. And Gideon asked
GOD to give him a sign that He would really do so.
Gideon put a fleece of wool on the ground and said
that if the dew fell on the fleece only, and all around it
was dry, then he should know that GOD would do as
He had said. "And it was so : for he rose up early
on the morrow, and thrust the fleece together, and
wringed the dew out of the fleece, a bowl full of
water." But Gideon's faith was weak, and he did not
feel quite satisfied yet. So he asked GOD to give him
one more sign. " Let it now be dry only upon the
fleece, and upon all the ground let there be dew.
And GOD did so that night; for it was dry upon the

fleece only, and there was dew on all the ground."
This was not only a sign to Gideon, it was a sign or
type to us all of the Incarnation of the Son of God.
You know, I hope, what that word "Incarnation"
means. It means being made flesh. So S. John says,
" The Word was made Flesh and dwelt among us."
It is in remembrance of this that we keep Christmas
Day. On this day the Son of God came down
silently and unobserved as the dew falling upon the
fleece of wool. He came first of all to the lost sheep
of the house of Israel. This is what is meant by the
dew first falling upon the fleece and leaving all the
ground dry. He came to His own, His chosen
people, but they received Him not. So then He
turned to the Gentiles, the other nations of the world,
and offered to them the heavenly dew of grace and
salvation, while the Jews who rejected and crucified
Him are left to this day dry and unbelieving. ' This
was shown by the fleece being left dry and the dew
falling on all the ground. The fleece becoming full of
dew in the first sign shows also the union of the two
natures of God and man in Christ. " Christ took
our nature, yet without sin, as the fleece, though it is
of the body, yet knows not the body's passions. That
heavenly rain came with gentle descent into the virgin
fleece, and the whole tide of Godhead hid itself in the
thirsty fleece of our flesh, till, wrung out upon the
cross, it poured forth in the rain of salvation over all
the lands."

But now let us turn from the sign to its fulfilment.
Let us think of that wonderful Birth of Jesus Christ
in remembrance of which we keep holy this day. On

the first Christmas Eve a poor couple were wandering
in the streets of Bethlehem, seeking shelter for the
night. But every place was crowded with the people
who had come from various parts of Palestine for the
great taxing or "census" that was ordered by the
Emperor of Rome. Joseph, a humble carpenter
from Nazareth, with Mary his Virgin-wife, sought
a lodging in the inn, but in vain. "There was no
room for them in the inn." So, wearied with their long
journey, they had to content themselves with the poor
shelter of a stable, and there, He who made heaven
and earth first saw with human eyes the light which
He had created. There, in a manger, among beasts
of burden, He was born who came to take away the
burden of our sins by bearing it Himself. Such a
wonder, surely, heaven itself has not beheld; GOD
Himself had come down upon earth, and this was the
way He was received !—none knew but Mary and
Joseph, and a few poor Shepherds, that GOD was
there in that lowly manger ; that that little helpless,
new-born babe, dependent on its mother for warmth
and food, was GOD Himself! Well might the bright
angel-messengers make the midnight skies ring with
their glad song of praise, "Glory to GOD in the
highest, on earth peace, goodwill towards men."
Secretly, silently as the sweet dew of dawn, CHRIST
appeared on earth that Christmas morning. Close
around Him, in the little town of Bethlehem, crowds
of men and women lay sleeping, and knew not that
their GOD was present in their very midst. And here,
away over the seas, in this land of England, our
heathen forefathers were living wild, savage lives,

hunting and feasting and fighting, worshipping gods whom they believed to be more cruel than themselves, and whose wrath they tried to turn away by human sacrifices. What would have been the thoughts of those wild, fierce men, if they had been told that in Syria, a land no further than the end of the Mediterranean sea, the Almighty Creator of the world was in man's flesh and true nature, lying a new-born babe in a manger? But they knew not. None knew but that favoured few; and yet He was there. You remember the story of Jacob's dream at Bethel? how he saw a ladder reaching from earth to heaven, and the angels of GOD going up and down it? Well, when he awoke, Jacob was frightened, and said, "Surely the LORD is in this place, and I knew it not! How dreadful is this place!—this is none other but the house of GOD, and this is the gate of heaven!" Would not the people of Bethlehem have said the same if their eyes had been opened to see who was amongst them? "Surely the LORD is in this place, and we knew it not."

Children, still according to His own most true promise, JESUS is with His Church "always even to the end of the world." His presence is very near us often when we little think it. When we go to Church, for instance, and meet together to worship Him, JESUS is in our midst. We cannot see Him, but He is there, for did He not say, "Where two or three are gathered together in My Name, there am I in the midst of them?" How careful this should make us always to behave reverently in the house of GOD!

Still nearer, children, you will be able to come into the Presence of JESUS when you have been confirmed.

Then you will be able to receive the holy Sacrament
of the Body and Blood of CHRIST.   Then, as the dew
fell upon the fleece, JESUS will come into you.   Under
the outward signs of Bread and Wine, you will verily
and indeed take and receive the Body and Blood of
CHRIST.   Oh, how close He will be to you !   You in
Him, and He in you !   There will be nothing to see
but a little bread and wine, as in Bethlehem there was
nothing to see but a little Babe; but under those outward forms faith sees JESUS present in human flesh
and blood.   Oh, if those who come carelessly and
unprepared to Holy Communion, and do not behave
reverently there, could see what the angels see, could
see who is really there—JESUS standing in the midst—
with what shame and confusion of face they would say,
"Surely the LORD is in this place, and I knew it not !"
But is not JESUS always near you ?   Can you never
come into His Presence except in Public Worship and
Holy Communion ?   Yes, dear children, He is always
near you, you are always in His Presence.   But not
quite in the same way.   I cannot explain this fully to
you; but here is an illustration that may help you a
little.   Suppose a clergyman is preaching in a great
church or cathedral to some two or three thousand
people; each one of that vast congregation is in the
presence of the preacher; his eye runs over them all.
But suppose one of that congregation stays after the
sermon to talk with the preacher in the vestry alone,
is he not more specially in the presence of the preacher
than he was just before when forming one of the congregation ?   If the clergyman could put his spirit into
that person's spirit so as to dwell in him and read his

inmost thoughts, would not that person be still more in the presence of the clergyman? Well, we are always under the eye of JESUS, but there are times when we can draw nearer to Him through the means which He has appointed. And the chief of these means is the Holy Communion. That holy Sacrament is the heavenly manna with which JESUS feeds His people in their journey through the wilderness of this world. You will remember how the manna was given to the children of Israel. " In the morning the dew lay round about the host. And when the dew that lay was gone up, behold, upon the face of the wilderness there lay a small round thing as small as the hoar frost upon the ground. And when the children of Israel saw it, they said one to another, It is manna;" that means, What is this? " for they wist not what it was. And Moses said unto them, This is the bread which the LORD hath given you to eat." Now JESUS CHRIST, who came down on Christmas morning like the dew from heaven, has gone up again into heaven ; but He has left us the blessed Sacrament of His Flesh and Blood to be our manna, our spiritual food, the bread for the strengthening and refreshing of our souls which the LORD has given us to eat. Dear children, JESUS who said, "Suffer the little children to come unto Me, and forbid them not," suffers you to come to Him now. In prayer you can speak to Him. In hearing and reading His Word, you can hear His voice speaking to you. In His house He is present to receive your worship, and He loves, as of old, to hear the mouths of babes and sucklings praising Him in the Temple. When you are confirmed JESUS will lay His hands upon you and bless you. And oh, look forward prayerfully and hopefully to the time when you shall be allowed to draw still nearer to JESUS and receive His very self into your souls and bodies in the Sacrament of His Body and Blood. No nearer can you draw to Him on earth. GOD grant that after this life you may enjoy the full unveiled glory of His Presence in heaven !

IX.

THE STAR IN THE EAST.

for Epiphany.

" Where is He that is born King of the Jews? for we have seen His Star in the east, and are come to worship Him."— S. Matt. ii. 2.

A LONG, long time ago, and a long way from here, in an Eastern land, there lived some men called Magi, or "wise men." These men were not Jews, but Gentiles, as all nations of the earth were called besides the Jews. They were however not idolaters, but believers in the true GOD. They spent a good deal of time in watching the stars, for it was a common belief in those days that many things were foretold by the stars about the fate of kingdoms and of men. The promise that MESSIAH, i.e., CHRIST, should come was known to many people on the earth besides the Jews,—and there was a general expectation that He would come about that time.

These wise men lived in the country where Nebu-

chadnezzar and Cyrus reigned, where Daniel prophesied, and where Esther was queen. So they very
likely knew a good deal about the prophecies of Messiah's coming, through the Jews, from whom their
forefathers must have heard them. From their country, too, Balaam came, and they had very probably
heard of his prophecy,—" There shall come a Star out
of Jacob, and a sceptre shall rise out of Israel," &c.
(Numb. xxiv. 17.)

At last their watching was rewarded. They saw a
new and wonderful star, and GOD in some way made
known to them that it meant that a King of the Jews
was born—*the* promised King. At once they set out
on a journey to Judæa to seek the newborn King and
worship Him. They take rich and costly presents,—
gold, incense, and myrrh, pack them and whatever
they thought they would need for the journey on the
backs of camels, and away they go, across wide de-
serts, fording swift rivers, going over steep mountain-
passes. What they suffered from heat, weariness, fear
of robbers and wild beasts, hunger and thirst, storm
and tempest, we know not. But they braved all dangers, bore all fatigue, with their one fixed object before them,—to see and worship JESUS.

At last they reached Judæa, and, naturally, they
made straight for Jerusalem, because it was the capital
of Judæa, just as, you know, London is the capital of
England. There they thought they would be sure to
hear where they might find this wonderful King. No
doubt they expected to find all Jerusalem in an up-
roar of excitement and rejoicing. What must have
been their surprise to find that no one knew anything

about it! Their story and eager questions only caused
trouble instead of joy. Herod "was troubled and all
Jerusalem with him." At last they get the informa-
tion they want. Herod, in fear and anxiety, sends for
the chief priests and scribes, and asks them where the
promised CHRIST was to be born. They search the
Scriptures, and find that the Prophet Micah had foretold that CHRIST should be born in Bethlehem.

Thus directed, again those faithful Gentiles set out
on their way, wondering no doubt that crowds of
Jews do not go with them. But no, the Jews do not
seem to believe or care at all about the matter. They
leave the wise men to go on alone.

All this time the star had disappeared. When it
had made known to them that the promised King had
been born in Judæa, it had done its work for the
time. They could find their way to Judæa without
its help. But now very likely they needed some fresh
sign to assure them that they had made no mistake,
as they might be tempted to fear when they saw the
unbelief of the Jews, and how little they cared about
it. So, though, no doubt, they had learned the way
to Bethlehem, GOD sent the star again to guide them.
"And when they saw the star, they rejoiced with
exceeding great joy." The cause of this exceeding
joy being probably that now they *knew* they were
right in spite of the unbelief of the Jews. Here was
a star, visible in broad daylight, going before them,
like the pillar of fire before the Israelites of old,
"until it came and stood over where the young Child
was." At such a wonder the wise men could doubt
no longer, if their faith *had* been shaken at all.

But there was to be another trial of their faith now. "And when they were come into the house, they saw the young Child with Mary His Mother, and——" what? turned back in disgust and disappointment, and set off back to their own land? was that what they did? No; but if they had not had strong faith in GOD, they might well have done so. For what had they found after all their long and toilsome journey? *This* the King of Whom such great things had been foretold? This poorly clad Baby on the lap of a poor Jewish peasant girl, in the humble cottage of a carpenter? Was this the King of the Jews? Surely there must be some mistake! We can fancy one of them going out again, and looking up at the star to be quite sure this was the spot. Yes, there it is, exactly over this very cottage. They needed all the assurance that GOD gave them by that wonderful star to keep their faith from failing. And it did not fail. "When they . . . . saw the young Child with Mary His Mother, they fell down and worshipped" not her, not them, but "Him:" and then we can fancy them unpacking their treasures, and presenting "unto Him" their gifts, "gold and frankincense, and myrrh."

Fancy the astonishment of Mary and Joseph at the arrival of this great cavalcade, the reverent behaviour of those grand, wise-looking old men, bowed with their faces to the ground before the Babe! How thankful they must have felt in their poverty for the costly gifts! How Mary must have "pondered in her heart" this fresh proof of the glory of her Divine Son!

First, the shepherds of Bethlehem had come, Angel-guided, to worship Him while yet lying in the manger; and now, these wise and rich men, evidently great personages, had been directed by a star to take that long journey, and had come and worshipped Him also. Thus early was it shown that, although He was sent first to "the lost sheep of the house of Israel," yet He had also come to be the SAVIOUR of the world. The prophecy was, at least in part, fulfilled which said, "The Gentiles shall com: to Thy light, and kings to the brightness of Thy rising." This was the first Epiphany, or manifestation of CHRIST to the Gentiles.

Now this story, besides the beauty and the wonder of it, has a special charm and interest for you and for me, children, because we are Gentiles. By so wonderfully guiding Gentiles to the new-born JESUS, GOD showed that He cared for all the nations of the earth, and not for the Jews only. He showed that all might come from the east and west, and north and south, and sit down with Abraham, Isaac, and Jacob in the kingdom of heaven. And so we ought to keep the Feast of the Epiphany with especial rejoicing and thankfulness. Without it we could not keep Christmas and Easter. They would have been Jewish Festivals, of deep interest to them, but nothing to us. We must surely be very thankful to GOD for guiding those first Gentiles to JESUS. And we ought to imitate those wise men by seeking Him with all our hearts, and worshipping Him also, bringing Him our best and choicest offerings, "ourselves, our souls and bodies, to be a reasonable, holy, and lively sacrifice to Him." We must have faith, as they had; a faith

that believes and perseveres in spite of all difficulties
and hindrances. And if we are in earnest, GOD helps
our faith as He helped theirs. We do not indeed
need a star to guide us to JESUS, nor any other wonderful sign, because *we* have plenty of light. GOD's
Word is a lamp unto our feet, and a light unto our
path. (Ps. cxix. 105.) His Church ever points out
the way to come to JESUS. The lives of thousands of
holy men and women and children "shine as the
brightness of the firmament, and as the stars for ever
and ever" to guide us to JESUS. And above all, there
is the inward guiding light of the HOLY SPIRIT ever
leading us, if we will but follow, to JESUS.

GOD grant, dear children, that you may so know
JESUS now by faith, that after this life you may have
the fruition, or enjoyment, of His glorious Godhead.

X.

THE CHILDHOOD OF JESUS.

for Epiphany Season.

"*And the child grew, and waxed strong in spirit, filled with
wisdom: and the grace of God was upon Him.*"—S. Luke ii. 40.

LET us think to-day of the childhood of our LORD
and SAVIOUR JESUS CHRIST. We are not told much
about Him as a child, or rather, we are not told about
that holy Child in many words, but we *are* told a great
deal in a very few words. If we put together what the

Bible tells us of the Child JESUS and what we know
from history to have been the ordinary life of a Jewish
child, we can draw a tolerably true picture of the child-
life of JESUS. And all that can be learned about
such a childhood as His must be well worth being
reverently treasured up and thought over by every
Christian child.

When Herod sought the young Child's life, Joseph,
warned by GOD in a dream, took the young Child and
Mary His mother and fled into Egypt, and was there
until the death of Herod. Herod died only a few
weeks afterwards. Then GOD sent an angel again to
Joseph, who appeared to him in a dream and told him
of Herod's death; so Joseph left Egypt, but was afraid
to go back to Bethlehem, for he heard that Archelaus,
who was cruel like his father, was king. Again GOD
directed him in a dream what to do, and accordingly
he went with JESUS and Mary to Nazareth, a little,
mean, out-of-the-way country town in Galilee, and there
the holy family lived. The place had an ill name,
we know, for in after years Nathanael asked, " Can
any good thing come out of Nazareth ?" But perhaps
this was one reason why GOD directed Joseph to go
thither, in order that it might be shown that it was
possible for a child to grow up in a wicked place, and
yet keep free from the wickedness of it. Some people
are apt to lay the blame, when they go wrong, upon
circumstances; and parents, whose children turn out
ill, will often say, in excuse for their own neglect and
mismanagement, that the children were led astray by
bad companions.

There must have been many bad, rude boys in the

streets of Nazareth; but Joseph and Mary, we may
be sure, took pains to keep the Holy Child from
their evil society, and JESUS would not join them in
their wicked ways. Here, then, in this wicked place,
in a poor carpenter's home, JESUS grew up from
infancy to boyhood, and all we are told about Him
until He was twelve years old is that He " grew
and waxed strong in spirit, filled with wisdom : and
the grace of GOD was upon Him." Still, this is a
great deal. How wonderful it is that He, Who is
Almighty GOD, should have become man; and that,
having resolved to become man, He should have
chosen first to be a baby and to grow up by degrees,
year by year, like other children! He might have
become at once a full-grown man, like Adam whom
He had created, and that would have been amazing
condescension. But He willed to come into the world
a helpless babe, and to pass into manhood, step by
step, through boyhood and youth, like us. His body
grew by food and warmth and sleep as our bodies
grow. He had also a soul like us, feelings and affec-
tions, as we have. He had, too, a spirit, a human
spirit, which could grow stronger and stronger. Our
spirit is that part of us " which makes us reasonable
beings ; it is by the action of our spirit that we think
of GOD, set Him before us, pray to Him, fear Him,
worship Him. It is, then, a great thing to say of any
child, and it could only be said of a good and holy
child, that he 'waxes strong in spirit.' It means, not
that he becomes taller, nimbler, cleverer, but that his
conscience becomes more and more formed as he
grows up, his will more steady in doing what is right

and avoiding what is wrong, his prayers to GOD more
earnest, his sense of GOD's Presence more keen, his
dread of sin stronger."[1]   The spiritual or religious life
of the holy Child JESUS grew stronger and deeper as
His body grew taller, and His Spirit kept His bodily
desires and the feelings of His soul in perfect subjec-
tion to the will and law of GOD.   And He was " filled
with wisdom."   Holy and heavenly wisdom kept flow-
ing into His human soul, so that, by-and-by, when
He was but twelve years old, we read of His astonishing the teachers in the Temple at Jerusalem by His
understanding and answers.   He was "wise unto that
which is good, and simple concerning evil."   (Rom.
xvi. 19.)   This wisdom comes from above, and "is
first pure, then peaceable, gentle, and easy to be
entreated, full of mercy and good fruits, without par-
tiality, and without hypocrisy."   (S. James iii. 17.)
And this wisdom, dear children, GOD will give to you
too, if you ask Him, for it is written, " If any of you
lack wisdom, let him ask of GOD, that giveth to all
men liberally, and upbraideth not ; and it shall be
given him."   (S. James i. 5.)   It is added that " the
grace of GOD was upon Him"—that is, the favour of
His Heavenly FATHER, and the precious influence of
His HOLY SPIRIT, Who was given to Him "without
measure," that is, in all His fulness.   On each Christian child, too, the grace of GOD rests.   At your Baptism GOD's favour was shown to you in the forgiveness
of sin for CHRIST's sake, and the gracious help of His
HOLY SPIRIT was given in some measure to you that
you might wax strong in spirit.

[1] Dean Goulburn, " Gospel of the Childhood."

As the holy Child JESUS grew up into boyhood, by-and-by, no doubt, He went to school, for the Jews had many schools, and thought a great deal of education. In Jerusalem, we are told, there were as many as three hundred and ninety-four schools. So, most likely, there was some sort of school at Nazareth, although it may have been a very humble kind of school, as inferior a school to those at Jerusalem as our old-fashioned village dame-schools were to the schools in most of our towns and villages at the present day. This may account for the scornful question of the Jews in after years, " How knoweth this man letters, having never learned?" We need not, I think, conclude that JESUS had never been taught to read the Scriptures and other simple learning, but only that the Jews looked with contempt upon such teaching as He would have had at such a place as Nazareth. But whether taught at school or by Mary His mother and S. Joseph in their cottage-home at Nazareth, we must be able to form a pretty good idea how He would learn His lessons. We must be sure that He was a very patient, obedient, attentive scholar, and that He tried His very best to understand and remember what He was taught, and that He gave His teachers as little trouble as possible. Will you, dear children, always try to imitate JESUS in this? And will it not make you take more interest in your Scripture lessons when you think that JESUS must have learnt the same stories of Joseph, Samuel, and David which you are taught? How eagerly JESUS must have learned the prayers and texts which His mother taught Him, or which He learned to repeat at school! There is a curious saying which was common at that time, "The world is only saved by the breath of the school-children," that is, by the prayers and holy words which their innocent lips repeat. And oh, dear children, how much might be done for the salvation of the world, if all the school-children in town and country really prayed the prayers they learn! How much was done for the salvation of the world by the prayers breathed from the lips of that holy school-child!

Then, think of that holy Child at play! For, no doubt, like all other children, He did play sometimes. There is no sin whatever in the *innocent* play of children. But is children's play always innocent? How often it ends in quarrelling, in angry words and blows! How often each child wants to have all its own way, and will not give way to the wishes of others! How often there is cheating or accusations of unfair play! How often children amuse themselves, and take delight, in teasing and torturing poor dumb animals! How often they play when they ought to be at work! Now, we must be quite sure that there was nothing of all this in the play of JESUS. He could play, happily and innocently, without being quarrelsome, or selfish, or unfair, or cruel to poor animals and insects, or playing at forbidden times. How much happier you would all be in school and at home if you always learned your lessons like the holy Child JESUS, and played as innocently as He played! You cannot, I know, imitate Him in your own strength. As the Catechism says, "My good child, know this, that thou art not able to do these things of thyself, nor to walk in the commandments of GOD, and to serve Him, *without His special grace;* which thou must learn at all times to call for by diligent prayer." Set before you, then, at all times, in school, and at play, in church and on your knees at private prayer, the example of the holy Child JESUS, and ask GOD very earnestly to give you His special grace, that you may, like JESUS, wax strong in spirit, and be filled with heavenly wisdom. Then I am sure that GOD will hear you when you pray, and will help you as you try to be like His Holy SON, and, as you increase in stature, you will increase, too, in wisdom and in favour with GOD and all good men whose favour and good opinion is worth having.

XI.

THE CRUCIFIXION.

ffor Goob ffribap.

"And they crucified Him."—S. Matt. xxvii. 35.

How much is told us in these four simple words, children ! What a story of pain and anguish, of Divine mercy and love is wrapped up in them ! They crucified JESUS ! What does that mean ? What is crucifixion ? Let us try to bring it home to our hearts on this "Good," but most sad and solemn " Friday." The time had come when it pleased our LORD JESUS CHRIST to put Himself in the power of His enemies. Fancy One so good and kind and gentle having enemies ! But He had, and cruel enemies too. Long had they sought His life, and at last one of His own disciples had, for a little money, betrayed Him into their hands. Guided by wicked Judas, they found JESUS in a garden where He had gone with His disciples to pray. He knew what was coming, and there, in the Garden of Gethsemane, He had been preparing for death, lying on His face in the moonlight, under the shade of the olive-trees, pouring out His very soul in such an agony of prayer, that a sweat of blood dropped from His body. The prayer was ended, the struggle was over, before His enemies came. He stepped forward to meet them, and let them take Him and bind Him and lead Him away. More easily than Samson He could have snapped the cords that bound Him ; like Elijah, He could have called down fire from heaven, and consumed those wicked men. But His love made Him willing to suffer for us, and He would not use His power. "He was led as a lamb to the slaughter, and as a sheep before her shearers is dumb, so He opened not His mouth." They led Him to Caiaphas, the high priest, and after a mock trial there, during which He was shamefully treated by those that held Him, and had the sorrow of hearing Peter, His loved disciple, deny that he knew Him, they led Him to Pilate, the Roman governor. Pilate could find no fault in Him, and wanted to let Him go ; but the mob kept on shouting "Crucify Him, crucify Him," and Pilate was afraid to displease them. So, after JESUS had been cruelly beaten with scourges (a horrible kind of whip), and mocked, and crowned with thorns, they led Him away to crucify Him. The cross, a great beam of wood with another beam across it, was laid upon His bleeding shoulders, and He was made to drag it along to the place of execution. He had no strength to carry such a load far, after all He had suffered that dreadful night, so they made one Simon, a Cyrenian, carry it for Him. When they came to the place called Calvary, or Golgotha, the soldiers stripped JESUS of His clothes, and, laying Him on the cross, drove great nails through His hands and feet, and then, raising the cross, planted it upright in the ground. This is what is meant by "They crucified Him." Oh, children, try to think of it as if you were really there and saw it. Don't you almost fancy you *can* see it? Look at that bleeding Form hanging nailed to the cross. Look up into that Face so bruised and swollen with blows. See how those sharp thorns are piercing His head. Ah, how the blood drops, splash, splash upon the ground from those wounded hands and feet. There He hangs, the children's Friend, He Who took the little ones in His arms and laid His hands upon them, and blessed them, and said, "Suffer the little children to come unto Me, and forbid them not." Have the children He loves so well no tears to shed for Him? There He hangs, and meekly bears it all, the suffering and the shame, for us, for you and for me. And, oh, children, remember that He Who hangs crucified there is Almighty GOD! How wonderful that He should have let men treat Him so. How awful that men should have dared to do it! And yet they were not at all frightened at what they had done. The Roman soldiers looked upon JESUS as a common criminal, like the two thieves who were crucified, one on each side of Him. They were quite used to such deeds and sights as this.

The chief priests and scribes and elders knew better, but, although they might have known that He was the CHRIST, the SON of GOD, they had hardened their hearts in unbelief, and only mocked Him as an impostor. What an awful scene for GOD the FATHER to behold ! what a fearful sight for the holy angels to look down upon ! The only-begotten SON of GOD nailed to the cross, and men mocking and jeering at His sufferings ! I cannot help thinking that a lightning flash must have come down from heaven upon those cruel men if it had not been stayed by that prayer which went up from the lips of JESUS, " FATHER, forgive them ; for they know not what they do." For JESUS' sake the FATHER spared them. Surely nothing else could have stayed His hand. Presently there came a great darkness, although it was mid-day. It fell like a veil, to hide from those cruel eyes the agonies of the SON of GOD.

Now, children, I have not told you half what happened there, the other words which JESUS spoke as He hung upon the cross, the dividing His garments by the soldiers, the title which Pilate put over His head, the scoffing of one thief, the penitence and faith of the other, the grief of the blessed Virgin His Mother, and of S. John and Mary Magdalene, the earthquake, and rending of the rocks, the opening of the graves of the sainted dead, and the torn veil of the Temple. All this would take too long to dwell upon now, and most of you can read it in your Bibles, as I hope you will, at home. I want you now to try to feel that JESUS suffered all this for *you*. Think how you would feel if cruel men were going to put *you* to all this torture. If you saw them preparing the scourges to lay upon your bare back, plaiting the thorn-crown to place upon your little head, getting the nails and hammer ready to drive through your little hands and feet. How you would cry and scream, and be in an agony of fright. And then think of JESUS coming, just as they were going to drag you away, and telling them that they might do it to Him instead, if they would only let you go. How thankful you would feel to escape such fearful pain, and yet how sad you would feel at seeing JESUS suffer in your stead! You could not go away and play and be merry, could you? And this is just what JESUS has really done. You and I deserved to be punished for our sins, and punished we should have been, and dreadfully we must have suffered, not on a cross, but in hell-fire for ever and ever. But the blessed SON of GOD came and bore all that suffering in our place. He " bare our sins in His own body on the tree" of the cross. He shed His precious blood that we might be forgiven. GOD *could* not have forgiven us if His SON had not died for us upon the cross. For, although GOD is merciful, He is also just, and it would not have been just in Him to have forgiven us. His justice required that sin must be punished. But His mercy found out this wonderful plan by which He could be just and merciful too.

Now, GOD *can* forgive us, and is most ready and willing to forgive us if we repent of our sins, and ask Him to forgive us, for JESUS' sake. He loves JESUS so much, that He cannot refuse us when we plead that precious blood shed for us upon the cross. This is why to-day is called " Good" Friday. Good, indeed it is for us that JESUS allowed Himself to be crucified for us. But we cannot, dear children, as some do, enjoy ourselves and make a holiday on this day, can we? No; because it makes us feel so sad to think of all that it cost JESUS to redeem our souls. We cannot be so selfish and hard-hearted as not to care what our dearest and best Friend suffered, so long as *we* get off free. He looks down into each child's heart to-day to see whether you feel for His suffering, whether you love Him for it, and, oh! He does want little children's love. He looks to see if you are sorry that you ever sinned against Him. And He looks down upon those crowds of thoughtless pleasure-seekers who fill the excursion-trains to-day, and crowd the beer-shops and places of amusement, without one thought of Him, and doubtless He says again, " FATHER, forgive them; for they know not what they do." That is it, I would fain believe it of most of them, they know not, they do not stop to *think*. Little children, too, are thoughtless; it is not easy to get their restless minds to stop and think for long together. But surely the sight of JESUS, GOD's dear SON, the children's Friend, nailed to the cross for *you*, will make even a child thoughtful.

Try, dear children, to keep Him in your thoughts all to-day. Try to think how good it was of Him to die for you. Try to love Him with all the warm love of your young hearts, and this day and always to show how thankful you are, and how much you love Him, by trying and praying to be and to do all that He would wish, and to keep from everything that you know would grieve His loving heart.

XII.

THE RESURRECTION OF CHRIST.

for Easter Day.

" And the angel answered and said unto the women, Fear not ye ; for I know that ye seek Jesus, which was crucified. He is not here ; for He is risen, as He said."—S. Matt. xxviii. 5, 6.

WHAT a short time between Good Friday and Easter Day ! and what a difference between the two days ! Good Friday the saddest day in all the year, Easter Day the brightest. On Good Friday how bare the Church looked, how sad were the hymns and chants ! It could not be otherwise when our hearts were full of the sufferings of JESUS. To-day what a change ! How bright the Church looks with flowers and decorations ! How glad and joyous are the services, how triumphant the Alleluias ! All speaks of joy, for CHRIST is risen from the dead. Think how sad the disciples of JESUS were on the first Good Friday. When they saw their dear Master " crucified, dead, and buried," all hope seemed gone, all the great things they had expected from Him seemed to have come to nothing. They "trusted that it had been He who should have re-deemed Israel," but now they did not know what to think. The chief priests and scribes seemed to have it all their own way, and evil triumphed over good. Poor broken-hearted men and women ! in that hour of sore trial and distress they had quite lost sight of the

often repeated promise of JESUS that on the third day
He would rise again. Oh, how glad they were when
by degrees they came to feel sure that JESUS had
indeed risen from the dead and was alive on earth
once more! If we at all shared their sorrow on Good
Friday, we shall be able to feel something of their joy
on Easter Day. Now, think of that first Easter morning. The Body of JESUS, you know, had been laid by
Joseph of Arimathea in his own new tomb, which was
not like our graves, but was a cave cut out of the rock.
The entrance to this tomb had been then blocked up
by a great stone, and the stone had been sealed. This
was done by stretching a cord across the stone door,
and fastening it to the rock on each side by sealing
clay. You will remember how, when Daniel was put
into the den of lions, King Darius sealed it with his
own signet and with the signet of his lords. The stone
which formed the door of the tomb of JESUS was
sealed in this way that it might be known at once if
the stone had been disturbed by any one and put back
again, for this could not be done without breaking the
seal. Besides this, some soldiers were set to watch
the tomb ; for the chief priests and Pharisees had a
better memory than the disciples, and they had not
forgotten that JESUS had said that He would rise again
on the third day. They did not believe that JESUS
would rise, but they pretended to be afraid that the
disciples would come by night and steal the Body and
give out that JESUS had risen from the dead. So
they had the stone sealed and put a guard of soldiers
there to make it impossible for any one to remove
the Body. But those foolish men might as well have

tried to stop the sun from rising, or the tide from coming up on the seashore. Just as the first rays of the rising sun were appearing over the Mount of Olives, JESUS passed quietly out of the tomb without disturbing the stone. The soldiers paced up and down, not knowing that now they were guarding an empty tomb, when all at once there was a great rumbling and shaking of the earth, a bright figure all in white, like a flash of lightning, darted down from heaven and rolled away the great stone and sat upon it. Oh, how frightened the soldiers were ! They shook from head to foot, and thought their last hour was come. But by this time there were other people there besides the soldiers. A party of women were coming from Jerusalem—Mary Magdalene, Mary the mother of James and Joses, Salome, and others, a sad little company, coming to have a last look at the body of Him they loved so well, bringing spices and ointments to embalm it. They did not know about the guard of soldiers and the seal, and had forgotten about the great stone. The difficulty had just occurred to them ; they were saying to one another, " Who shall roll us away the stone from the door of the sepulchre?" They, too, must have felt the earthquake, and been frightened at the glorious appearance of the angel. But the angel called out to them, " Fear not ye; for I know that ye seek JESUS, Which was crucified. He is not here, for He is risen, as He said. Come, see the place where the LORD lay." These good women had no cause for fear, because they were seeking JESUS. The angel did not tell the soldiers not to be frightened. I dare say most of you children have heard stories about ghosts, and you would perhaps be afraid to go into a churchyard at night. Now, it would not be true to tell you that there are no such things as ghosts or spirits, for there are, and very likely there are some always near us, but we cannot see them. They do not often appear to men now, if ever; and if you were to see any being from the world of spirits, or an angel of GOD, you see *you* need not be frightened. The angel had come to *help* those poor women, to roll away the stone for them, and tell them that JESUS was risen; and he spoke very kindly to them. He did not *hurt* even those wicked soldiers, he only frightened them away so that the women might come and look inside the tomb and see for themselves that the Body of JESUS was no longer there. How surprised and glad they must have been! And when they went into the tomb they found two bright angels there, who spoke to them and reminded them that JESUS had said to them, "The Son of Man must be delivered into the hands of sinful men, and be crucified, and the third day rise again." And they remembered His words, and "departed quickly from the sepulchre with fear and great joy, and did run to bring His disciples word." Afterwards they saw JESUS Himself, and so in time did all the disciples, and became witnesses to all men that JESUS had truly risen from the dead. And, ever since, the Church has kept Easter Day with great joy and thankfulness, and, because JESUS rose on the first day of the week, we keep Sunday, instead of Saturday, holy; the Jewish "Sabbath" was changed to "The LORD's Day."

Now let us see why *we* should rejoice and be glad

on Easter Day, why "the LORD is risen from the dead"
is such glad tidings for *us*.

First, the resurrection of JESUS—that is, His rising
from the dead, *proves* that He is the SON of GOD.
How were people to know that JESUS was the SON
of GOD? He said that He and GOD the FATHER
were one, that He had been alive before Abraham,
that He had come down from heaven, and that those
who believed in Him would be saved. These were
great things to say. If they were true He must be
equal with GOD, must be GOD. But any one might
say these things : how could people tell if they were
true? There were His miracles, His wonderful teaching, His holy life. But these might show Him to be a
great prophet ; nothing more, people might think.

Well, JESUS had promised the Jews a great sign. As
Jonah had been swallowed by the fish and had appeared again the third day, so JESUS would die and be
buried "in the heart of the earth," and would come
forth alive the third day. Also, our LORD had told
His disciples again and again that He would rise again
the third day ; and on another occasion He had said
to the Jews, "Destroy this temple and in three days I
will raise it up," meaning by the temple His Body. So
you see, if JESUS had *not* risen, His own promised sign
would have come to nothing, and people, even His
own disciples, must have felt that JESUS was not the
SON of GOD, however much He may have thought that
He was. But JESUS did rise from the dead. No one
raised Him up as He had raised up Lazarus. JESUS
raised Himself from the dead. Could a mere man
do that? Now it is clear that *all* JESUS said of

Himself is to be believed—is most certainly true.   He is the Resurrection and the Life, He is our Prince and SAVIOUR.   He is, as S. Paul said, "declared to be the SON of GOD with power—by the resurrection from the dead."

Then, again, because JESUS rose from the dead, we know that He will come again to be our judge.   So S. Paul told the Athenians, GOD "hath appointed a day in the which He will judge the world in righteousness by that man whom He hath ordained ; whereof He hath given assurance unto all men, in that He hath raised Him from the dead."   And is it not good news that we shall have as our judge Him who loved us so well that He died to save us ?

Then, again, because JESUS rose from the dead we know that GOD accepted the sacrifice which JESUS offered for us.   JESUS "died for our sins, and rose again for our justification."   S. Paul told the Corinthians that if CHRIST had not risen they were yet in their sins, no pardon, no salvation for them.

Lastly, because JESUS rose again, we know that we shall rise again.   He will change our bodies and make them like His glorious Body.   Our dear friends who sleep in JESUS will live again, we shall see them once more.

So, you see, dear children, how much depended on JESUS rising from the dead, how much it has to do with our salvation.   Well may the joy bells ring on Easter Day, and the Churches be decked with flowers. Well may we sing with all our hearts, " JESUS CHRIST is risen to-day, Alleluia."   " As in Adam all die, even so in CHRIST shall all be made alive."   And remember that "He died for all, that they which live should not henceforth live unto themselves, but unto Him which died for them and rose again;" and that you should "reckon yourselves dead indeed unto sin; but alive unto GOD through JESUS CHRIST our LORD."

XIII.

THE CONQUEROR'S TRIUMPH.

𝔣𝔬𝔯 𝔄𝔰𝔠𝔢𝔫𝔰𝔦𝔬𝔫 𝔇𝔞𝔶.

"Thou hast ascended on high, Thou hast led captivity captive: Thou hast received gifts for men; yea, for the rebellious also, that the Lord God might dwell among them."—Ps. lxviii. 18.

ASCENSION Day! Who ascended to-day? Whither did He ascend? Why did He ascend? These are questions that a thoughtful child may ask. And when you learn that JESUS CHRIST ascended to-day, and that He went up on high, above, and "*far* above, all heavens," and that He went up for *us*, to receive gifts for us, and to appear in the Presence of GOD for us, then, perhaps, a thoughtful child may ask further, Why then do so many people take no notice of such a day? And I can only answer, Because, poor souls, they know not, or from unbelief care nothing about it.

But never mind about other people's neglect, I want you, children, to learn about the Ascension of JESUS CHRIST, and to see what a blessed and joyful day it is.

You know that when our LORD JESUS CHRIST rose
from the dead, He did not at once ascend into heaven. For forty days He stayed on earth, showing
Himself at different times and places to His Disciples.
Then, at the end of the forty days, JESUS led His
Apostles out from Jerusalem as far as to Bethany, and
while His hands are lifted up to bless them, see, He
rises up from the earth before their astonished eyes,
and goes right up into the sky. Up, up, He goes
until they can scarcely see Him, and then a bright
cloud came and He was lost to their sight. No
human eye might trace Him farther in His glorious
upward flight; no human ear might hear the triumph
songs with which the angels welcomed the conquering
King, victorious over death and the grave.

Yet stay, hundreds of years before, David had heard
in spirit those angel songs. Long, long ago, he had
sung them to his harp,—"Lift up your heads, O ye
gates, and be ye lift up, ye everlasting doors, and the
King of Glory shall come in. Who is the King of
Glory? The LORD strong and mighty, the LORD
mighty in battle. Lift up your heads, O ye gates;
even lift them up, ye everlasting doors; and the King
of Glory shall come in. Who is this King of Glory?
The LORD of Hosts, He is the King of Glory."

How sweet must have been the voices of those
angel choirs, how splendid the triumphant progress of
the mighty Conqueror through the skies up to the
glorious Throne of GOD! Earth has had its great
men, its conquering heroes, welcomed home with
splendid triumph and great rejoicings after their
glorious victories; but earth has never seen such a

triumph, has never honoured such a hero. Earth?
Why even heaven itself had never before known anything like it. All earthly triumphs have been but
faint shadows of that one. It was a splendid triumph,
a grand procession, when David sang that sixty-eighth
Psalm, from which the text is taken. It was a prophetic
procession, dimly shadowing out the triumphant Ascension of CHRIST. The Ark of GOD was being
carried to its rest at Jerusalem, after it had returned
from the land of the Philistines, and GOD had, as it
were, caused it to conquer its enemies and work its
own deliverance by the wonders it brought upon the
idols of Philistia. The singers went before, and the
minstrels followed after, in the midst were the damsels
playing on timbrels. The white-robed Levites bore
it and guarded it. The priest in his beautiful vest-'
ments received it, and David, arrayed in white, danced
and sang and played on his harp in an ecstasy of holy
joy. The Ark was a type of CHRIST, and the procession was a faint image of the triumphant Ascension
of CHRIST.

We may find a type, too, though of course not an
intentional one, in the old Roman triumphs. The
Romans used to welcome home their conquering
generals with the most magnificent triumphs. When
a general returned home after a great victory, or number of victories, all the city kept holiday; every one
turned out to see the show; the streets and altars and
images of the gods were hung with wreaths of flowers.
The magistrates went to welcome the conqueror, and
headed the procession in their white and purple robes;
then came trumpeters; then were carried the spoils

taken from the enemy, coins, jewels, arms and armour, pictures, statues, and other works of art, costly stuffs, and so on.   Then boards with the names of the con- quered cities and countries painted on them, models of the places themselves, and pictures of the rivers or hills of the territory added to the great Roman em- pire.   Then flute-players, white oxen for sacrifice with gilded horns and garlands hung about them, the priests walking beside them.   Next were carried the standards and crowns of the enemy, then came the captives, kings, queens, or beaten generals, with their armies, all in chains.   After them the conquering hero himself, riding in a chariot drawn by three white horses, dressed in a flowered tunic and robe em- broidered with gold.   He had a sceptre in one hand, ·a branch of bay in the other, and a wreath of bay on his head.   Behind him stood a slave holding a golden crown over his head, and it was the duty of the slave to whisper, lest his head should be turned with all this splendour, " Remember that thou art a man."   A much needed caution, for you will remember what happened to King Herod when he allowed the people to flatter him by crying out, " It is the voice of a god, and not of a man."   The general's little children were allowed to ride in the chariot with him, and very pleased and proud they were, I expect, with all the grandeur about them.   Behind the general came his grown-up sons in other chariots, and his officers, then the cavalry first and after them the infantry carrying spears adorned with bay leaves, and shouting, " Io Triumphe !"   The whole procession went rejoicing on up to the temple of their chief god, Jupiter, where the oxen were sacrificed, an offering was made from the spoil, and the bay wreath was taken off the victor's head and laid in the idol's lap. Then the general sat down to a great feast with all his friends, and was escorted to his home with torches and music at night. A house was given to him, and he was for life an honoured man in Rome. It was a grand sight, but it was spoilt by an act of great cruelty and bloodshed, for some of the wretched captives were slaughtered, and the others became slaves for ever.

How different from the triumph of JESUS, for He came not to destroy men's lives, but to save them, not to make men slaves, but to set them free from the slavery of sin.

> "Conquering kings their titles take
> From the foes they captive make :
> JESUS, by a nobler deed,
> From the thousands He hath freed."

The captives whom JESUS led in His triumph were the enemies of man,—the Devil, that old serpent whose head He had bruised, and death and the grave, the wages of sin. The gifts which JESUS received were not for Himself. What He received as man, the rewards of His sinless human life, victorious over temptation and the tempter, JESUS received not for Himself, but for us. For us He received that glorious gift of GOD, eternal life. For us He received the LORD and Life-giver, the HOLY SPIRIT with His seven-fold gifts, Whom He sent down upon His little band of faithful followers, His infant Church, on the Day of Pentecost, that He, the HOLY SPIRIT, the LORD GOD, might dwell among them, and that He Himself might, by the SPIRIT, be present with His Church, "always, even to the end of the world," as He had promised. Even for the rebels, His enemies, JESUS received these precious gifts, that by the grace of the HOLY SPIRIT they might be turned from rebels into faithful subjects, and so lay hold on eternal life. On the very Day of Pentecost three thousand of these rebels were turned into penitent believers at the preaching of S. Peter; they laid down their arms of rebellion, and were baptized and added to the Church of JESUS CHRIST. And how many thousands and hundreds of thousands since!

Children, JESUS looks down upon you from His glory throne on high. No little child is beneath His notice. He loves and cares for you all, just as He loved little children when on earth, for He is "JESUS CHRIST, the same yesterday, to-day, and for ever." He never changes. He looks down to see what use you each make of the blessed gift of the HOLY SPIRIT Which He won for you by His Crucifixion, Resurrection, and Ascension. To you at your Baptism the HOLY SPIRIT was given to make you able to resist sin. He will be given to you in greater measure the more you use and pray for His help. At your Confirmation He will be given to you still more abundantly by the laying on of the Bishop's hands, if you come earnestly wishing to be confirmed and strengthened in all goodness. And, if you rightly use that gift, and do not grieve and quench the HOLY SPIRIT by wilful sin, you will receive the crown of eternal life, and have your part in that glorious triumph on the

day when JESUS returns with His holy Angels to lead
the hosts of His redeemed ones up through the
golden gates to dwell for ever with Him in the
courts above.

XIV.

THE COMING OF THE HOLY GHOST.

For Whitsun Day.

" *Ye shall receive power, after that the Holy Ghost is come upon
you; and ye shall be witnesses unto Me.*"—Acts i. 8.

THESE are some of the last words spoken by our
LORD JESUS CHRIST before His Ascension into Heaven.
When He had spoken these words, " while they beheld, He was taken up; and a cloud received Him
out of their sight." After our LORD had risen from
the dead, He did not keep with His disciples always
as He used to do. He came and appeared suddenly
among them, and as suddenly vanished out of their
sight, and no one knew whither He went. This went
on for forty days. He was preparing them for His
final departure. And now when He was going away,
never to return in bodily presence on earth until the
last great day, He comforted them by repeating His
promise that the Comforter, the HOLY GHOST, should
come to be with them when He was gone. He had
told them before His Crucifixion that it was expedient,
or good, for them that He should go away, for that, if
not, the Comforter would not come. They could not

understand this. They could not see how any one could make up to them for the loss of their dear Master and Friend. Still, when they had seen Him go up before their eyes into Heaven, they remembered His promise, and waited patiently, day after day, praying that what He had promised might come to pass, and not doubting that it would come to pass. They had not to wait long. Ten days after JESUS had ascended, the disciples were all gathered together into one place, probably the large upper room, where JESUS had eaten the Passover with the twelve, and instituted the blessed Sacrament of Holy Communion. It was the Day of Pentecost, the same day as our Whitsun Day, and about nine o'clock in the morning. The Jewish Day of Pentecost was a sort of Harvest Festival. It was also called the Feast of Weeks, because it took place a week of weeks, seven weeks, or forty-nine days after the Passover. Hence its name Pentecost, or Fiftieth, because it was the fiftieth day after the Passover.

So Whitsun Day is seven weeks after Easter. A great many Jews from all parts of the world came to Jerusalem for this great festival. Well, it was on this day, the Day of Pentecost, when the disciples, a hundred and twenty in number, were gathered together praying, that our LORD's promise was fulfilled. All at once a great rushing sound was heard, like a mighty wind. No wind was felt. Nothing was blown about. Only the rushing sound was heard. At the same time a strange sight was seen. A pillar of flame appeared overhead, which parted into smaller jets of fire resting upon the head of each one. Yet no one was burnt.

Not a hair was singed, as, you remember, GOD spoke to Moses out of the midst of a bush which burned with fire and yet was not consumed, not a leaf crackled, not a twig was scorched. The noise and the flame were the signs of the coming of the HOLY GHOST.

The HOLY GHOST is GOD, He is a Spirit, and has no shape or form which can be seen by men. The noise and the flame were only signs of His Presence. But the disciples had another proof that He had come. They all felt lifted out of themselves, as it were, filled with a new power, and they could not help beginning immediately to praise GOD, and this, too, in languages which they had never learned or known how to speak before. " They were all filled with the HOLY GHOST, and began to speak with other tongues as the SPIRIT gave them utterance." The rushing noise was so great that it was heard all over the city, and a great crowd came running together to see what was the matter. Jews who had come from a number of different countries, and who spoke all kinds of different languages, were there, and think how surprised they must have been to hear the disciples talking in all those different languages ! Fancy how astonishing it would be if all of you were suddenly to begin saying prayers or singing hymns, some in French, some in German, some in Italian, others in Spanish, and so on ! The Jews who had come from foreign countries understood what the disciples were saying, but they could not explain how it was that they were able to do it. But the Jews, who lived in Jerusalem, and who did not know those foreign languages, thought that the disciples were talking nonsense, and said that they must be drunk.

They might have thought how unlikely it was that men should drink wine so early in the morning, a thing which even the greatest drunkards would not do, much less such sober, good people as the disciples were. Then S. Peter stood up and explained to them what had really happened. He told them that this was exactly what their own prophet Joel had long ago foretold. Then he spoke of the resurrection of CHRIST, and showed them how David had foretold *that* in the 16th Psalm, and declared that he and all his fellow-disciples were witnesses that JESUS *had* risen. You know "a witness" is one who speaks of what he has seen and known, and the disciples had *seen* JESUS after He had risen from the dead, and knew Him. S. Peter went on to tell them that JESUS was now exalted at the right hand of GOD, and, having received of the FATHER the promise of the HOLY GHOST, had shed forth this which they now saw and heard. And he ended by telling them that they might now know for certain that the same JESUS whom they had cruci- fied was both LORD and CHRIST. This cut them to the heart. The HOLY GHOST blessed the words of S. Peter and enlightened the minds of the Jews, so that they saw and felt the wickedness of which they had been guilty. They asked the Apostles what they should do. Then S. Peter told them that they must repent of their sins and be baptized, and then their sins would be forgiven, and they, too, would receive the gift of the HOLY GHOST. And when he had spoken to them for some time longer and taught them, three thousand of them were baptized on that very day. What a curious sight it must have been ! There

were no Christian churches built yet, no fonts for Holy
Baptism, so all those people had to be baptized in the
open air. There was no river or pool in Jerusalem
deep enough for three thousand people to be dipped
into the water, so water must have been poured upon
their heads in the Name of the HOLY TRINITY. What
wonderful power had so changed the hearts of those
three thousand men? Seven weeks ago many of them
were crying out for JESUS to be crucified. Some of
them, perhaps, had stood among the crowd around
the cross and joined in mocking JESUS as He hung
dying there. Certainly all of them but a little while
ago hated the very name of JESUS of Nazareth. Now
these same men were eagerly seeking to join the body
of disciples, the infant Church of JESUS; now they
were being baptized into the Name of JESUS and of the
FATHER and of the HOLY GHOST. Who had brought
this wonderful change about? GOD the HOLY GHOST
had done it. What had changed S. Peter, too, and
the other disciples? For a change had come over
them also. Seven weeks ago S. Peter denied JESUS
through fear, and all the disciples forsook Him and
fled. Seven weeks ago the Apostles were hiding, probably in the same upper room where they now were,
for fear of the Jews. *Now* here was S. Peter standing
up boldly with the others before all the Jews bearing
open and public witness to JESUS! Who had given
the disciples such courage? Again, GOD the HOLY
GHOST had done it. He had changed the timid disciples into brave witnesses for CHRIST; He had
changed the unbelieving and persecuting Jews into
humble and teachable believers; as the Baptismal

water was poured upon their heads, they passed into
a new state of life, a state of salvation, they were
" born again of water and of the SPIRIT."

Children, the same HOLY GHOST Who came down
upon the infant Church of JESUS on that day never
went away again. He has continued in the Church
ever since, and is working in it now. It is He who
pricks men to the heart when they have done wrong,
and leads them to repentance and faith. He touches
sinners' hearts by the preaching of the Gospel, and
gives power to the sacraments and ordinances of the
Church. He does not come with rushing sound or
pillar of flame ; but He is still given to children when
the hands of the Bishop are laid upon their heads in
Confirmation, if children come in earnest to that holy
Sacramental Rite. There, at the Altar step, they
receive power by the coming upon them of the HOLY
GHOST, power to be witnesses to JESUS by faithful
holy lives. At your Baptism your bodies became
temples of the HOLY GHOST. He came to be with you,
your dear Friend and Guide and Helper, the loving
SPIRIT, to lead you forth into the land of righteousness.

Oh, children, think often of JESUS, and try to love
Him more and more ; but think often, too, of the
HOLY GHOST, the Spirit of JESUS. Think of Him as
a Friend, ever near, even within you. Ask Him to
help you. Pray for Him to dwell in you ever more
and more. Are your prayers cold, and is it hard
to keep your thoughts from wandering away ? The
SPIRIT will help your weakness if you ask Him. Are
you afraid of being laughed at and teased if you try to
do right, and refuse to join others in what you know

is wicked? The same HOLY SPIRIT who made S. Peter so brave will give you courage too, if you ask Him. Is it hard to remember and obey what you are told? hard to do your lessons carefully? hard to conquer a hasty or sulky temper? hard to be brave enough always to speak the truth? In all your difficulties, in all your struggles to do right, GOD the HOLY GHOST will always help you, if you ask for His help. He loves you more tenderly than even your mother does. You grieve Him when you do wrong. He is pleased with you when you ask Him to help you, and if you will let Him be your Guide, He will lead you safe to Heaven.

XV.

ANGELIC PROTECTION.

for S. Michael and All Angels.

" The angel of the Lord encampeth round about them that fear Him, and delivereth them."—Psalm xxxiv. 7.

I WILL begin by telling you a story, or rather by reminding you of one which, I dare say, most of you already know. In the time of Elisha the prophet, when Jehoram son of Ahab was king of Israel, the king of Syria made war upon Israel, and in secret council with his generals decided upon the best places to make his attack, so as to take the king of Israel by surprise. But each time Elisha sent and warned the king of Israel of the plans of the Syrians. This vexed

and alarmed the King of Syria very much, for he
thought that there must be some traitor in his council
who kept warning the King of Israel. "He called his
servants, and said unto them, Will ye not show me
which of us is for the King of Israel?" And then one
of his generals told him that there was no treachery
among them, but that Elisha made known to the King
of Israel the most secret intentions of the Syrian king.
Then the King of Syria gave orders to find out where
Elisha was, and hearing that he was in a place called
Dothan, he sent thither horses and chariots and a
great army to fetch Elisha, dead or alive. Now this
was very silly of the King of Syria, because he might
have known that if Elisha was able to put the King of
Israel on his guard, he would be able to take care of
his own safety as well. And we shall see that he did so.

One morning early, Elisha's servant went out, and
was terribly frightened at finding that the city was
surrounded by a large army of Syrians. He ran and
told Elisha, in great distress, and cried, "Alas, my
master, how shall we do?" But Elisha was not at all
frightened, and only answered, "Fear not; for they.
that be with us are more than they that be with them."
Then Elisha prayed to GOD to open the young man's
eyes, that he might see. "And the LORD opened the
eyes of the young man; and he saw: and, behold,
the mountain was full of horses and chariots of fire
round about Elisha." Elisha had seen them all the
time, and so he was not afraid. He knew that the
angel of the LORD was encamped round about him,
because he feared GOD; and when the young man
saw them too, no doubt he feared no longer. Then

Elisha prayed to GOD to smite the Syrians with blind-
ness ; and GOD did so, and all that mighty host
became a confused crowd of poor, helpless, blind men,
and Elisha was able easily to lead them to Samaria,
where the King of Israel was with his army. But he
would not let the King of Israel hurt them. He
taught the king a lesson of mercy to those whom GOD
had put into his power. So the King of Israel gave
the Syrians plenty to eat and drink, and sent them
back to their king.

There are many other stories in the Bible which
show the truth of the text, that "the angel of the
LORD encampeth round about them that fear Him,
and delivereth them." When the Assyrians, in the
days of Hezekiah, encamped against Jerusalem, "the
angel of the LORD smote in the camp of the Assyrians"
an hundred and eighty-five thousand men. When
Daniel was cast into the den of lions, GOD sent His
angel and shut the lions' mouths, that they should not
hurt him. S. Peter was delivered out of prison by an
angel. And there is good reason to believe that one
of the holy angels is appointed by GOD to watch over
each Christian child.

Our LORD said of little children that "in heaven
their angels do always behold the face of My FATHER
which is in heaven." And when S. Peter was delivered
from prison, and went and knocked at the door of the
house where his friends were assembled together praying for him, they thought at first that it could not be
Peter himself, but "his angel," i.e. his guardian angel.
Even heathen have believed that each man has his
good "genius," or angel. It was also the belief of

the Jews, except that sect of them called Sadducees, who said that there was neither angel nor spirit. Now, I have found that this thought of the guardian angels has been a great comfort to timid little children who were afraid to be left alone in the dark. And perhaps there may be some timid children among you. Well, whenever you feel afraid, think of your guardian angel. What makes some children so frightened in the dark? They cannot *see* anything to frighten them; but they keep *thinking* of frightening things, and fancying danger where there is none! So they are frightened, not at anything that is really there, but at their own timid thoughts and fancies. Now, why should not a child think of its guardian angel, *instead* of thinking of ugly and horrible things? The ugly and horrible things are not really there, they are only imaginary; but the guardian angel *is* really there. You cannot see him; but neither can you see the things which you are frightened at.

You think, and think, about frightening things until you really believe them to be there; why should you not think, and think, about GOD's protecting love, and His good angel watching near you, until you really believe him to be there? Surely it is happier and nicer, as you lie awake, to think sweet, comforting thoughts of the holy and beautiful angels of GOD, than to be frightening yourself with all sorts of fancied terrors! Oh, if your eyes were opened, as were the eyes of Elisha's servant, and you could see that bright angel watcher! You might be frightened at him at first, he is so glorious, so brightly shining; but he would say to you as the angel who was sent to Daniel, and

that bright one who appeared to the shepherds at
Bethlehem, " Fear not ;" he would tell you that he
was sent to be always near you, to take care of
you, and you would get over your fear at his great
glory and brightness, and feel that you never could be
frightened again with such a protector at your side.
You cannot see him, but he is there ; and the dangers
that you fear are not there. But perhaps some timid
child may be thinking, " No doubt God gives His
angels charge over *good* children to take care of them;
but I am not always good ; I am often very naughty ;
will God's angel take care of me ?" But, my dear
child, who is " always good ?" And the text does not
say " the angel of the LORD encampeth round about
them that are always good ;" but " round about them
that fear Him," that is, those who love and reverence
Him, and believe in and obey Him, *as a rule*, although
they may sometimes,—as who does not ?—fall into sin.
And I hope that you do, on the whole, " fear God,"
and try to do His will, and that, when you have done
wrong in any way, you are sorry and are careful to
ask God to forgive you for His dear Son's sake, before
you lie down in your bed. Then you may be quite
sure that God hears your prayer, and forgives you at
once ; and the angel-watcher is sure to be there, at
your side, glad that although you did wrong you repented of your wickedness, for " there is joy in the
presence of the angels of God over one sinner that
repenteth." But if a child should be so sinful and
wicked as to lie down at night in a sinful, unrepentant
temper, without being sorry and without prayer, I do
not say that that child could comfort itself with the

thought of the protection of the angel-watcher; although GOD is so good and kind even to the unthankful and evil, and so unwilling that any should perish, but that all should come to repentance, that no doubt He would take care even of that wilful child, and give it time to come to a better mind.

So, dear children, if you wish to be brave, and to drive away foolish fancies and frightening thoughts, think often of your mighty protector, your bright guardian angel. Pray to your FATHER in Heaven, that as His holy angels always do Him service in Heaven, so by His appointment they may succour and defend you on earth ; and *believe* that GOD hears your prayer. Do not doubt that He *does* appoint His angels to watch over His little ones, and that He will not let any harm happen to you. It is wrong to give way to fear of mere fancied dangers which have no real exist-ence. It is distrust of your FATHER'S loving care ; and He wants His children to " put their whole trust in Him."

I will end with two verses of Bishop Ken's beautiful Evening Hymn, which you may like to learn to say over every night when you lie down to sleep.

"O may my Guardian, while I sleep,
Close to my bed his vigils keep ;
His love angelical instil ;
Stop all the avenues of ill.

"May he celestial joys rehearse,
And thought to thought with me converse ;
Or, in my stead, all the night long,
Sing to my GOD a grateful song."

XVI.

THY KINGDOM COME.

For the Day of Intercession for Missions.

" Thy kingdom come."—S. Matt. vi. 10.

THIS day has been chosen by the Archbishop of Canterbury as a day of prayer for GOD's blessing on Missions to the heathen. I believe that GOD hears the prayers of little children, and loves to answer them, as much as the prayers of grown-up people. So I want to say a few words to you, dear children, to explain to you *why* you should pray, and *how* you should pray for the heathen, and for good men to go and teach them the way of salvation.

By the goodness of GOD you have all been born in a Christian land. As soon as you were able to learn, you began to be taught about GOD and His dear SON JESUS CHRIST, and you are taught hymns and prayers to say. Before you could speak or understand anything you were brought as little babies to the font and baptized in the Name of the FATHER, and of the SON, and of the HOLY GHOST. You were made members of CHRIST, children of GOD, and inheritors of the Kingdom of Heaven.

But in some other parts of the world, hundreds and thousands of little children are born and grow up without knowing anything of the true GOD and JESUS CHRIST. Is it not sad? Yes, and there was a time when England was a heathen country. There were

no churches or schools, and no clergymen to teach
people about GOD. Poor little children were often
burned alive, numbers of them shut up in a great sort
of wicker basket and burned as an offering to their
gods. But missionaries came and taught the people
about GOD and JESUS CHRIST. And by degrees,
after many years' hard work, they made many of the
people Christians. But still the greater number remained heathens until a good man named Augustine
came with some companions and converted the king
and a great many of the people to Christianity.

They were sent by S. Gregory, a good Bishop of
Rome, and this is how S. Gregory came to send the
missionaries to England. One day, before he was
bishop, he went into the market-place at Rome, and
saw a number of prisoners, men, women and children,
whom the Romans had taken in war. Among them
he saw some pretty fair-skinned, blue-eyed children,
and he stopped and asked who they were. He was
told they were Angles, as the English were then
called. So he said they would be not Angles but
Angels if only they were Christians. After asking a
few more questions about them and their country,
S. Gregory wanted to go himself as a missionary to
England. But the people at Rome loved him so much
that they would not let him leave them. Still he
never forgot the poor heathen English, and when he
was made Bishop, he sent S. Augustine and forty
others as missionaries to England. So they set out,
but on their way they heard such dreadful stories of
the cruelty of the savage English, that they were afraid,
and S. Augustine went back to Rome to ask S. Gre-

gory if they need go among such savage people. But
S. Gregory would not hear of his turning back. So
S. Augustine started again and went to England, and
GOD blessed his work so much that a great many of
the English gave up their wicked idolatry and became
Christians. S. Augustine became the first Archbishop
of Canterbury, and in time all England became
Christian.

But this was the work of many, many years. And
now there are many parts of the world where the
people are just as savage, and know as little about
GOD as our heathen forefathers. Not near half the
people in the world are Christians. There are parts
of the world, as large as England and larger, with
only one or two missionaries. So you see there is
great need for many more missionaries; and we
who enjoy the blessing of Christianity in our own
land ought to feel pity for those who are in heathen
darkness, and we should pray to GOD to send more
missionaries to teach them.

Missionaries have to live a hard life, and brave
many dangers. They often go to very unhealthy
countries, as good Bishop Mackenzie did, who died
of fever in Africa when he had only been out there a
little more than a year. Sometimes the people to
whom they go are very savage and cruel, and the
missionaries are murdered,—so good Bishop Patteson
only a few years ago, was killed by the heathen in one
of the Melanesian islands near Australia. Those who
go as missionaries have to leave home, and friends,
and comforts, and to face many difficulties and dis-
couragements which we in England have little idea of,

besides often risking health and life. Only the love
of JESUS, and of the poor heathen who do not know
Him, can make men who might be happy and com-
fortable at home, give up all and go to live among
heathen and teach them. Only GOD can put it into
their hearts to wish to go, and give them grace to
persevere in such a work.

So you, dear children, are asked to join in praying
to GOD to do this, to raise up earnest, CHRIST-loving
men, full of faith and of the HOLY GHOST, to give
themselves to this work. Think of the poor little
children in those far off lands, how happy they would
be to learn what you are so often taught. They are
so glad when a missionary comes and teaches them;
they take such pains to learn. Then, when they grow
up, many of them become missionaries themselves,
and spread the knowledge of the Gospel of CHRIST
throughout their own nation.

Who can tell the good that may be done by our
prayers together to-day? Suppose one earnest missionary is raised up in answer to prayer; he goes to
Africa, or India, or elsewhere, and gets the people
to let him teach their children the Christian religion
and baptize them. Suppose *one* child becomes a true
believer; he goes and talks to his parents and friends
about CHRIST, and tells them the good news he has
learned. One here, another there, believe and are
baptized, and each convert becomes in his turn a
teacher of others. Who can tell how many hundreds
and thousands may become earnest Christians in a
few generations even though our prayers to-day were
to gain one more missionary, and that missionary

were to lead to CHRIST but one heathen child! What a glorious thing to have been privileged to have a share in such a work! And you can share in it by your prayers. Only remember you must *mean* the words you say. The people of Japan, an island near China, have what is called "a praying machine," it is a wheel fixed on an axle in an upright post; every person who, in passing, twirls the wheel round, is supposed to obtain credit in heaven for a certain number of prayers, according to the number of twirls the wheel has made. Is not that silly? Well, those poor people know no better.

> "But are you sure that we ourselves
>   Do not sometimes kneel down to pray,
>   Repeating words, while all the time
>   Our thoughts are wandering far away?
>
> "Then, while we laugh at poor Hindus'
>   And heathen Tartar's foolish prayers,
>   Let us be careful that our own
>   Are wiser, more sincere, than theirs.
>
> "Now, children, go; and when you pray,
>   Entreat the good and gracious LORD
>   To send to each dark heathen land
>   The Lamp of Truth—His Holy Word."

Pray earnestly with feeling hearts, thinking of those hundreds and thousands of poor heathen children growing up without knowing anything of Him Who said, "Suffer little children to come unto Me and forbid them not, for of such is the kingdom of heaven." Do not think that you are too little, and your prayers too faint and weak to do any good. All together you can do a great deal. Did you ever hear of the coral animals? they are tiny little things without heads or hands to work with, and yet they are the builders of islands big enough for trees to grow, and men to live upon. There are 290 of these coral islands in the Pacific Ocean, with an area of 20,000 square miles! All this the work of some of the feeblest and smallest of GOD's creatures. Think of that, and don't fancy that you are too small and weak to help in doing a great work.

> "Little deeds of mercy,
>   Sown by youthful hands,
>   Grow to bless the nations
>   Far in heathen lands."

Now I have tried to show you, children, *why* you should pray :—

Because of GOD's mercy to you in causing you to be born in a Christian land.

Because England was once a heathen land, and GOD raised up men to come as missionaries to our forefathers.

Because it is so sad to think of the numbers of poor children growing up in heathen darkness.

Because GOD only can put it into the hearts of men to give up so much that they love, and brave the hardships and dangers of a missionary's life.

And I have tried to show you *how* you should pray,—earnestly, meaning what you say, and hoping that GOD will do what you ask,—not saying words of prayer, like praying machines, while you do not really care whether GOD hears or not.

You have learnt too what to pray *for*,—more missionaries, more labourers in GOD's harvest. Pray also for the poor children, that they may be willing to learn about JESUS.

GOD give you praying hearts, dear children, and bless you while you pray "Thy kingdom come."

XVII.

JESUS AT A FEAST.

ꬡor a Scbool ꬡeast.

" Blessed is he that shall eat bread in the kingdom of God."— S. Luke xiv. 15.

I AM going to speak to you about a feast, and as your thoughts are full of your own school-feast, which I hope you will soon be enjoying, I think that what I say will be interesting to you. Once upon a time one of the chief Pharisees made a great feast, and JESUS CHRIST was one of those whom he invited to it. I am sorry to say that the invitation was not kindly meant. The Pharisee had a bad object in it. It was the Sabbath-day, and there was a man there who had the dropsy, and the Pharisee and his friends wanted to see whether JESUS would heal this man on the Sabbath, which they thought a very wrong thing to do. So they watched JESUS. JESUS did heal the man of his dropsy, for *He* knew that it was not wrong to do works of mercy and love on the Sabbath, and He wanted to teach them so.

When JESUS had healed the man, He put this

question to them, "Which of you shall have an ass
or an ox fallen into a pit, and will not straightway pull
him out on the Sabbath-day?" And they had nothing
to say, for they knew that if their own property was in
danger, they would not think it wrong to save it on
the Sabbath-day. Then our LORD noticed what a
scramble there was among the guests to get the best
places at the feast, so He told them that people should
not push themselves forward, but take any seat they
could get, and then, perhaps, the master of the feast
would tell them to go into a higher place; but if he
noticed them seating themselves in the best places, he
would be likely to turn them out to make room for
some one of more consequence, and they would feel
very much ashamed. So JESUS taught them a lesson
of humility. Do not some children need to be taught
the same lesson? I think I have sometimes seen
children scrambling for the best places at school
feasts, and Christmas trees, and even in Church.

Next our LORD turned to the Pharisee who had invited Him, and told him that he ought not to ask
only rich people to his feasts just that they might invite him in return, but that he should sometimes
make a feast for the poor, who could not ask him
back again, and then GOD would reward him at the
resurrection of the just. One of the guests hearing
this, said, " Blessed is he that shall eat bread in the
kingdom of GOD." This was a common saying among
the Jews. They thought of the Messiah's kingdom
as a great feast. And so in one sense it is, and it is
often spoken of in the Bible under the figure of a
feast, but it is a feast of spiritual blessings, a feast for

the soul, not for the body. What the man said was good and true enough, but the spirit in which he said it was not good. JESUS CHRIST read the man's thoughts and saw that he was, like most Pharisees, quite contented with himself, and thought himself quite sure of a place at the heavenly feast. So our LORD, knowing what was passing in the man's breast, told him a little story about a man who made a grand feast and asked a great many people to come to it. When all was ready, he sent his servant to tell them. But they all began to make excuses. When the servant told his master, he was very angry, and told the servant to go and call in the poor, and maimed, and lame, and blind, and to fill his house with such guests as these, for he said, " None of those which were bidden shall taste of my supper."

Our LORD meant by this story that the kingdom of GOD had come, and all things were now ready. John the Baptist had told the Jews so, our LORD Himself had told them, and He had sent His twelve apostles and seventy other disciples all over the land to make it known and to invite the Jews to come in. But they all made excuses for not believing the good tidings and for refusing the invitation, so our LORD warned them by this story that the blessings of His. gospel which they put from them, should be offered to the poor despised Gentiles, who *would* accept them, while the Jews would be shut out. So far from this man being as sure as he thought himself of a place among those who would eat bread in the kingdom of GOD, he was at that moment shutting himself out by his pride and unbelief. It is easy to *talk* religiously,

to say as this man said, "Blessed is he that shall eat
bread in the kingdom of GOD," but what is the use of
that if the kingdom of GOD has already come nigh
unto us and we are, on one excuse or another, reject-
ing its blessings ?   The kingdom of GOD means the
Church of JESUS CHRIST.   If we use its blessings
and privileges rightly now, we shall have the enjoyment of still greater blessings in it hereafter.   We can
eat bread in the kingdom of GOD now, that is, get
food for our souls from the Word and Sacraments and
other means of grace which CHRIST has provided for
us in His Church.   Some people refuse this food.
They make all sorts of excuses for not going to
Church or to Holy Communion, for neglecting prayer
and reading their Bible, and so on.   But if we rightly
use these blessings now, we shall hereafter go to
heaven and have fulness of joy for ever there.   I say
if we *rightly* use them, for many go to Church, and
even to Holy Communion, and yet are none the better.
You know some people do not thrive on even good
and wholesome food, because they can't digest what
they eat, and so we cannot be the better for the
spiritual food of GOD's Word unless we not only
"read, mark, and learn," but "inwardly digest it,"
that is, unless it becomes part of ourselves, enters into
our character, and influences our daily life.   We must
be " doers of the word and not hearers only."

Truly "Blessed is he that shall eat bread in the
kingdom of GOD," and this, my children, you will be
able to do in a very special and true sense when you
are Confirmed.   For then you will be admitted to the
LORD's Table and the LORD's Supper, at which your

Catechism tells you we receive "the strengthening and refreshing of our souls by the Body and Blood of CHRIST." By this Spiritual Food your souls will be fed and nourished, just as by bread and wine our bodies are strengthened and refreshed. Truly blessed are they who, with a real hunger and thirst after righteousness, partake of this bread in the kingdom of GOD! But that you may be able rightly to use and to enjoy this and the other blessings of His Church, you must open your hearts, children, to CHRIST. He comes and stands and knocks at the door of your hearts and asks you to open your hearts to Him, and love Him, and trust Him. He says, "If any man hear My voice, and open the door, I will come in to him, and sup with him, and he with Me." If we love JESUS and want to love Him more and more, then we feel a pleasure in the services and Sacraments of His Church, in reading and hearing of Him, in prayer, and in everything that brings Him near to us and us to Him, and helps us to know Him better. And unless we can enjoy the blessings and privileges which we now have in His kingdom on earth, how can we be fitted to enjoy the blessings of His kingdom in Heaven? And oh! what blessings, what joys will be there! Children, you look forward to your school-feasts with eager and joyful expectation Do you ever look forward to the feast of heavenly joys? As the time draws near for your school-feast, how anxious you are that nothing may happen to disappoint you! How you hope that you will be found to have attended school often enough to be allowed to come, that you may not get ill, that it may not rain. What a terrible disappointment if any of these causes prevented your enjoying it! And yet, after all, how'soon your treat is over! how little it matters to you a day or two after whether you were there or not! But the heavenly Feast! oh, if you should be shut out from that! For the joys of that Feast never cease. It goes on, for ever. There will be no sickness, nor bad weather, nor anything there to spoil your enjoyment of that Feast. *There* no want, or sorrow, or pain will be known; there will be "fulness of joy and pleasures for evermore."

JESUS invites you all to this blessed Feast which He has prepared, and the chief joy of which is His own dear presence there. He calls you by the voice of teachers, friends, the priests of His Church, calls you by the voice of His HOLY SPIRIT within you, calls you to feast on all the blessings which even in this life are to be enjoyed in His Kingdom, and hereafter yet greater joys than these. He calls you each one. His invitation is free to all. " The Spirit and the Bride say, Come." No one can say of this Feast, " I cannot come because I have not been asked." No one need be shut out but those who don't care to come and those who come too late. Come, children all, come in time, and mind you be not too late. " They that seek Me early," said GOD, " shall find Me."

XVIII.

THE OLDEST RIDDLE.

" I will now put forth a riddle unto you." . . . . *" Out of the eater came forth meat, and out of the strong came forth sweetness."*
—Judges xiv. 12, 14.

THIS is a very old riddle, children, the oldest riddle in the world. Can you guess it? Very likely some of you know the answer, but others do not. Perhaps some of you do not know what a riddle is? Well, it is a puzzling question or story or saying, of which we have got to try to find out the real meaning. A parable is a kind of riddle, so is a fable. Our LORD taught people by parables to make them think. It is so hard to get people to think, even grown-up people, about Divine truths.

Now, before I say more about this oldest riddle, I should like to say something about the person who put forth that riddle. I wonder how many of you know who he was. He was a wonderful man, and his life was a kind of riddle. It had a meaning in it which it takes a little thinking to find out. Indeed, the Old Testament is full of riddles, and for the answers to them we must look in the New Testament. Well, the man who put forth this riddle was Samson. Now try and guess the riddle of Samson's life, see if you can make out Whom he was made to represent. Before Samson's birth an angel came and told his mother that she should have a son. Afterwards the angel came again, and told Samson's father too. When

Samson was born, we read that "the child grew, and the LORD blessed him." Samson fought with a lion, and overcame it. He delivered his own people from their enemies. His own countrymen, the Jews, gave him over bound to the enemy. When Samson was shut up in Gaza and watched over by the Philistines, he rose up at midnight and tore down the gates of the city and went away with them on his shoulders, and carried them to the top of the hill that is before Hebron.

Samson was three times tempted to betray the secret of his strength, and three times resisted the temptation. Samson was betrayed into the hands of his enemies by Delilah, whom he trusted, and she betrayed him for a bribe of money. Samson's enemies had no power over him until he put himself into their power by laying aside his great strength. And, lastly, Samson was brought forth, cruelly treated and blinded, and exposed to the mockery and ridicule of the Philistines, and then he took the two main pillars of the house in his outstretched arms and bowed himself, calling upon GOD, and the house fell. "So the dead which he slew at his death were more than they which he slew in his life." Now I think you all see the answer to this riddle. You will say Samson was a type of CHRIST.

An angel came to tell the Blessed Virgin that she should have a wonderful Son. Afterwards an angel appeared to Joseph in a dream. When JESUS was born, we read that "the Child grew and waxed strong in spirit, filled with wisdom, and the grace of GOD was upon Him." JESUS went about destroying the

works of the devil, and overcame him who is called
"the roaring lion." JESUS came to deliver His people
from their enemies. JESUS was bound and given up
by the Jews into the hands of the Romans. When
JESUS was shut up in the sepulchre and watched by
the Roman soldiers, He rose up at night and went
forth. JESUS was three times tempted by Satan, and
three times overcame him. Although here a difference
is to be noted; Samson replied to Delilah's temptations
by three lies, but CHRIST replied to the temptations
of Satan by three sayings from the Scripture of truth.
The enemies of JESUS had no power over Him until
He laid aside His power, but not sinfully, as Samson
did, and gave Himself up to them. Lastly, JESUS was
mocked and blindfolded in the soldiers' hall. And,
as "Samson was exposed to the ridicule of the people;
his arms stretched out, grasping the two main pillars of
the house; their triumph, to all appearance, complete;
their enemy, to all human sight, at their mercy, so
JESUS was lifted up to the reproach and contempt of
the people : His arms stretched out upon the wood of
the cross; His hands grasping the two main pillars of
the house of Satan, viz., Death and Sin; and He
'cried with a loud voice and bowed His Head,' not
in the weakness of death, but with all the strength of
full life; for He cried with a loud voice to show that
no man took that life from Him, but that He laid it
down of Himself, that He had power to lay it down,
and power to take it again. 'He bowed Himself with
all His might, and the house fell.' Fell upon Satan,
and overwhelmed him; fell upon Death, and destroyed
him; fell upon the grave, and burst its bars." "O

Blessed SAVIOUR, our better Samson !" exclaims Bishop
Hall; "Thou didst conquer in dying, and triumphing
upon the chariot of the cross, didst lead captivity
captive. The law, sin, death, hell, had never been
vanquished, but by Thy death. All our life, liberty,
and glory spring out of Thy most precious blood !"

We have seen that the true answer to the riddle of
Samson's life is to be found in our LORD's history.
Now let us see how Samson came to put forth that
strange riddle, " Out of the eater came forth meat, and
out of the strong came forth sweetness." Samson was
raised up by GOD to destroy the Philistines, a people
who always hated the Israelites, and were oppressing
them very much before Samson delivered them. And
Samson went and married a Philistine woman. This
seems a strange way of beginning, but it was ordered
by GOD, and led to events which gave Samson a good
reason for punishing the Philistines. Once, when
Samson was going to pay a visit to his intended bride,
he went into a vineyard, probably to pick some grapes
to refresh himself on the way. A fierce young lion
sprang out upon him. But Samson was too strong
even for the lion, for GOD the HOLY SPIRIT gave him
strength, and, though quite unarmed, he tore the lion
open by main strength, and left him dead. He did
not tell any one, not even his father or mother. By-
and-by Samson came past that place again, as he was
going with his father and mother to take his wife, and
he turned aside to see the dead body of the lion. He
found that a swarm of bees had made a hive of the
skeleton of the lion, so he took some of the honey
and ate it, and when he joined his father and mother

he gave them some of the honey, but he did not tell them where he had found it. This was the meaning of the riddle which Samson put to thirty of the Philistines who came to the wedding-feast. They would never have guessed it ; but they threatened Samson's wife that they would burn her if she did not find it out and tell them. So she coaxed Samson to tell her the answer to the riddle, and she told the guests. And, just before the seven days were gone which Samson had given them in which to guess the riddle the guests came to him, and said, " What is sweeter than honey? what is stronger than a lion ?"

" Out of the eater came forth meat, and out of the strong came forth sweetness." And may we not say that there is another answer to that riddle, and that it means that GOD often causes what is nourishing and good for our souls to come out of what is in itself hurtful and dangerous? that GOD often brings forth to His people out of strong temptation the sweetness of victory and peace ? Sickness and pain and affliction are in themselves "eaters," devourers of our happiness, but GOD turns them into means of grace and blessing to us if we take them rightly. So David said, " It is good for me that I have been afflicted, for before I was afflicted I went astray, but now have I kept Thy Word." What is this but "out of the eater came forth meat ?" Then, what a terrible thing is temptation ! How strong some temptations seem ! But if by the grace of GOD we stand firm and resist the devil, he flees from us, and how great the sweetness of the calm and thankful joy that follows ! The sweeter, the stronger the temptation was. See what

S. Paul writes, "We glory in tribulations also : know-ing that tribulation"—that is, trouble of any kind—"worketh patience; and patience, experience; and experience, hope; and hope maketh not ashamed; because the love of GOD is shed abroad in our hearts by the HOLY GHOST, which is given unto us." What is this but good out of evil, meat out of the eater, sweetness out of the strong?

GOD grant you, dear children, to overcome the lion that walketh about seeking whom he may devour. GOD give you strength by His HOLY SPIRIT to rend him asunder, and ever through life may you return good for evil, love for hate, blessing for cursing, and, at last, taste the sweetness of those who have come out of strong temptation, great tribulation, and have washed their robes and made them white in the blood of the Lamb !

XIX.

BEAUTIFUL CHILDREN.

" For who maketh thee to differ from another? and what hast thou that thou didst not receive? Now if thou didst receive it, why dost thou glory, as if thou hadst not received it ?"—I Corinthians iv. 7.

As I look upon the faces of these children, I notice that no two of them are exactly alike. Between some there is a very great difference. Some faces are very pretty, others are—I will not say ugly, for a child's face is very seldom ugly, except when it is disfigured by angry passions—but not so pretty. Some of you again, are bright and clever, while others are not so. Now I want to show you all that those who are pretty and clever ought not to be vain and boastful, because as GOD gave you your good looks and quick wits, it would be very silly and very wrong in you to be vain, as if you had made yourselves. And it would be very wrong too to look down upon and despise others who are not so good-looking or clever, because GOD made them what they are. If the Master has given you five talents, you are not to look down upon another child to whom GOD has only given one talent. GOD gives talents, good looks, quick wits, and so on, to be used for His glory and in His service, and not to please our self-love and vanity. The plain-featured, uninteresting looking, slow, and awkward child, who is doing his or her best to please GOD by the right use of such powers as GOD has given, is much more beautiful in the sight of GOD than a pretty or clever child who is always seeking to be admired and noticed, and, forgetful of the Giver, is foolishly vain of the gifts. "For man looketh on the outward appearance, but the LORD looketh on the heart."

There was once a little boy whom GOD had made very pretty and bright looking. Every one who entered the house noticed the child and spoke of his beauty. One day a gentleman called upon business, and being engaged in conversation, did not pay that attention to the child to which he was accustomed, and which he now began to expect as his due. The vain little fellow made many efforts to attract notice, but not succeeding he at last placed himself full in front of the gentleman, and asked, " Why don't you see how beautiful I be ?" Now was not he a very silly little boy ? and do not you think that GOD Who sees the heart, saw so much ugly vanity there, that it quite spoilt all the beauty of that little face ? We all love to look upon what is beautiful, whether it be child or woman, or flower or animal, valley or river ; but we should never forget Who gave them their beauty. We all love beauty, but if we see in a face which GOD made lovely a look of pride and self-admiration, that look spoils the fairest face and gives it an ugly expression. It repels us instead of attracting, and makes it unpleasant instead of pleasing to look upon. We feel this even in the case of flowers. Who does not love the violet, and the lily of the valley, and the primrose ? These are prime favourites with most of us. And why ? Not merely because they are beautiful, but because they seem to us also to be so modest, and lowly, and retiring, while some other flowers, equally or more richly hued, *seem* to be more showy, and, as it were, to thrust their beauty on our notice.

Well now, I want you to think in this way. Suppose some one has praised your good looks, and said, " Oh, what a pretty child !" or has praised your cleverness, and said, " That is a very quick child," and so on,—say to yourself, Why should I be vain and pleased at this praise and admiration ? Who made me pretty, if I am so, or cleverer, if it be true, than others ? Who made me to differ from another ? What have I that I did not receive ? Why should I glory as if I had not received it? Give GOD the glory, do not take it to yourself, you have no right to it. You remember the story of Herod, how on a certain occasion he was gorgeously apparelled, and when he addressed the people they shouted " It is the voice of a god and not of a man," "and immediately the angel of the LORD smote him, because he gave not GOD the glory : and he was eaten up of worms, and gave up the ghost."

Now think of our LORD JESUS CHRIST, how careful He was to give to His FATHER all the glory. He said, " The SON can do nothing of Himself, but what He seeth the FATHER do : for what things soever the FATHER doeth, these also doeth the SON likewise." You cannot see the least trace of vanity or self-admiration in JESUS, and He tells us to learn of Him, for He was "meek and lowly in heart." We do not know what His human face was like, whether it was what men call beautiful or not. Certainly He patiently allowed that face to be spat upon, and buffeted, and bruised; until, as Isaiah prophesied, " His visage was so marred more than any man, and His form more than the sons of men :" and " He hath no form nor comeliness, and when we shall see Him there is no beauty that we should desire Him." And no doubt He bore all that disfigurement to rebuke our love of admiration, and to make an atonement for our foolish and sinful vanity. And because He humbled Himself, GOD has highly exalted Him, and that Face is now so gloriously beautiful, that man cannot look upon it, and when S. John saw Him in a vision after His Ascension, he "fell at His feet as dead." Some day *we* may hope to "see the King in His beauty," and to gaze upon Him with undazzled eyes ; and more than this we are taught to expect, for S. John says, "We know that when He shall appear, we shall be like Him, for we shall see Him as He is." What a wonderful prospect ! to be like JESUS in His glory and His beauty ! How will the most lovely child or woman wonder *then* that she could ever have been tempted to be vain and conceited of a beauty so far inferior to that of the lowest angel, of the least of those in the kingdom of GOD ! There will be differences and varieties there of form, and feature, and beauty, for " as one star differeth from another star in glory, so also is the resurrection of the dead." But none will be vain of their beauty, none will look down on others as less beautiful, none will seek admiration for themselves. All will be ever mindful Who made them to differ from one another, and will lose all thought of self in adoring Him Who is the Author and Giver of all that is beautiful and good.

Try then, dear children, to be humble and modest, seek the help of GOD the HOLY SPIRIT to make you like JESUS in meekness and lowliness of heart; then you will be beautiful in the sight of GOD, and He will make you glorious in beauty in the sight of men and angels hereafter. If you are prettier than some of your companions now, if your friends tell you so, or if you fancy yourselves to be so, beware of pride, beware of the sin of robbing GOD of His glory by seeking for yourselves the praise that belongs to Him, your Maker. As the beauty of a precious stone depends very much upon its setting, try to match and adorn your outward beauty by "the ornament of a meek and quiet spirit, which in the sight of GOD is of great price," and then, when the outward beauty, which is but "skin deep," fades away, as fade it must, the inner beauty will still be there, and the faded bloom of youth will be replaced by a glory and loveliness which will never pass away, but through the ages of eternity will reflect the surpassing beauty of Him Who is "chief among ten thousand and altogether lovely."

XX.

A LION IN THE WAY.

" The slothful man saith, There is a lion in the way; a lion is in the streets."—Prov. xxvi. 13.

WE seem to see here a picture of a lazy man lying in his bed, unwilling to get up and go about his proper business. There he lies, turning from side to side like a door which turns on its hinges, but never leaves them (ver. 14). His conscience tells him that he ought to shake off his laziness and get up, but he makes all sorts of excuses, and fancies he sees all sorts of difficulties in the way. He says, "There is a lion in the way; a lion is in the streets." Of course this is an absurd and fanciful excuse. How could he know there was a lion in the way? He had not been out of his bed to see. Besides, it was not likely, or even possible that there should be such a danger. For lions do not walk about the streets, and if they do venture near the dwellings of men by night, when "the sun ariseth, they gather themselves together, and lay them down in their dens" (Psalm civ). So the danger was imaginary, the excuse false and foolish, and he knew it ; but any excuse, however fanciful, will serve a lazy man's turn.

Now I am afraid that there are lazy children as well as slothful men and women, children who don't like to get up when they are called, and are cross and fretful if made to get up. These lazy children have their "lions in the way ;" they are " so sleepy," or "it is so cold," or "so dark," or they "think they have got rather a headache," and so on. Now, lying in bed and thinking about the difficulty of getting up is the very worst plan. The difficulty gets bigger and bigger, and the lion seems to roar dreadfully and to lash his tail, and show his teeth and claws, and it seems impossible to face him. But jump out briskly and cheerfully at once, without stopping to think about it, and the lion turns out to be only a bush after all, or a chained lion that can do no harm ! You remember the story of Christian and the lions in the " Pilgrim's Progress ?"

Christian was making his way to the Palace Beautiful, in his journey to the Celestial Country, when he met Mistrust and Timorous running away from it because they had seen two lions in the way. Christian was rather frightened at first at this news, but, plucking up his courage, he went on till he came in sight of the lions. Then Christian was very near turning back,

for the way was narrow, and he did not see how to
pass them unhurt; but the porter called to him that
the lions were chained, and he went on safely. Well,
many people see lions in the way, especially of anything they don't much like to do. Very often they
are only imaginary lions. If they are real lions, GOD
either shuts their mouths, as in the story of Daniel, or
chains them.

Let us think of a few lions in the way of little
children doing what they ought to do.

I have spoken of lions in the way of getting up in
the morning, and pointed out how they may be made
harmless. Now, what is the first thing you do as soon
as you are dressed? the last thing you do before you
undress to get into bed? Pray to GOD, I hope.

I trust that no lion in the way will ever make you
give up your morning and evening prayer. So long
as little children are at home, the only lion likely to
come in the way of these is too much haste to get
into bed at night, and too great unwillingness to leave
it in the morning. You have it in your own power to
chain up these two lions, and mind you put the chain
on, or they will eat up your words as soon as they
leave your lips. I mean, they will make you hurry
your prayers, and say them without thinking to Whom
you are speaking, and then your words of prayer will
never reach the ear of GOD.

But if you go away from home to school, or service,
may be you will not have a room all to yourselves
in which to say your prayers. Others will share
your room with you, school-fellows or fellow-servants.
And these, perhaps, have not been taught, as you

have, to begin and end each day with prayer; or,
having been taught, they have grown careless, and
given it up. Then comes a terrible lion in the way.
You are afraid that they will laugh at you if they see
you kneel down to pray, so you are frightened, and
tempted to give up your prayers, or to say them
secretly in bed. But, oh, children, do not play the
coward. Think of Daniel. He, although he knew
that, if he was seen praying to GOD, he would be cast
into the lions' den, went on bravely, just as he had
been used to do, praying three times a day to the
LORD his GOD, caring not who saw him. And he *was*
cast into the den, but the LORD sent His angel and
shut the lions' mouths, so that they did not hurt him.
And I have heard, not once or twice, of boys who
bravely fought this lion in the way, by kneeling down
boldly before their companions, night after night, and
morning after morning, until those who began by
mocking, at last came to kneel down and pray too.
One of these boys is now a Bishop of the Church of
GOD in England.

Then I have found among the children of the poor
a great many lions in the way of their coming regularly to school. Sometimes a baby is the lion which
stops a child. Sometimes it is harvest-time; sometimes hay-making; sometimes, being wanted to run
errands; sometimes, masting, or picking up acorns
for the pigs; sometimes whortleberry-gathering; sometimes picking over apples, or getting up potatoes;
sometimes bad shoes, or chilblains, or rainy days. It
is wonderful what a number of fierce, roaring lions
stop the way of children coming to school. And if a

child turns back or stays at home for each one of these savage beasts, his attendance at school is very irregular indeed, and he grows up very ignorant of many things very important for him to know. I do not say but what, now and then, the difficulty may be a very real lion in the way, whose mouth won't be shut, and who cannot be chained. But surely most of these lions, if walked boldly up to, would vanish away. Most of these difficulties might be got over, if only there is a good will. Some children, at any rate, do get past these lions somehow, and why should not others?

I might point out certain lions in the way of break-ing off a bad habit, or making up a quarrel; but I don't want to tire you. There are, in short, lions in the way of doing everything that is good and useful and right, and the longer you stop to look at them and shrink from facing them, the fiercer they seem, and the more dreadful sounds their roar. But only go manfully on, and, not stopping to think of difficul-ties, do at once what you know to be right, and, when it is done, you will wonder what has become of the lion. You will often find that he has skulked away, sulkily clanking his chains, or turned into a lamb or a bush.

After all, dear children, the real lion is the Devil, who, S. Peter tells us, "as a roaring lion, walketh about, seeking whom he may devour." He is always in the way of everything that is good and holy and pure and right. If you stop to listen to him, that wicked devil will make you fancy you see such diffi-culties and dangers in the way of whatever you ought to do, that you will never have courage to set about it. Don't stop to listen to him. Listen to GOD, Who tells you, " Resist the devil, and he will flee from you." Yes, from *you*, little and weak though you may be. Never turn back for difficulties. Think this rather. It must be very good and right for me to do this, just *because* the devil puts such difficulties in my way. If it did not matter much whether I did it or not, he would never take so much trouble to stop me.

Reason thus, dear children, and lions in the way, instead of making you turn back, will only make you feel that you must press on the more earnestly and resolutely. Put your trust in GOD, that is, take the shield of faith. Hope for His protection, that is, put on the helmet of salvation. Be upright and sincere, that is, "having your loins girt about with truth, and having on the breastplate of righteousness." Be peaceable and gentle to those who laugh at you, or are unkind, so will your feet be "shod with the preparation of the Gospel of Peace." Take "the sword of the Spirit, which is the Word of GOD ;" and, believe me, difficulties and dangers will disappear, lions will flee out of your way, or you will fight and overcome them in the strength of the Lion of the tribe of Judah, JESUS CHRIST.

XXI.

THE SYRO-PHŒNICIAN WOMAN.

"Lord, help me."—S. Matt. xv. 25.

OUR LORD JESUS CHRIST had been for more than a year in Galilee teaching, and healing, and going about doing good. But in spite of all His goodness and kindness to the people, they would not believe in Him and love Him. He stood at the door of their hearts and knocked, but they would not open their hearts to Him and let Him in. Scribes and Pharisees came from Jerusalem bringing accusations against JESUS, and stirring up the people against Him. So at last JESUS sorrowfully left them.

Wearied with His labours, and finding that they would not let Him do them good, He went away to rest awhile in that part of Galilee which borders on Phœnicia. Phœnicia was a heathen country, the chief towns of which were Tyre and Sidon. The people who lived there were Canaanites, one of the ancient nations of Canaan who were the enemies of GOD's people.

JESUS did not go among them to teach and to heal, because He had come first to the Jews, GOD's chosen people, although He meant the offer of salvation through Him to be made afterwards, in His own good time, to *all* the nations of the world, called " Gentiles," to distinguish them from the Jews. But His time for this had not yet come, and He did not *enter*

the country of Phœnicia, but remained in that part of
Galilee which was next to it.

Now in Phœnicia, somewhere in the neighbourhood
of Tyre and Sidon, there lived a poor woman who
had an afflicted daughter. This poor child was pos-
sessed with a devil. People who were afflicted in
this terrible manner were not necessarily bad people.
They were sometimes dumb, or blind, and subject to
fits, and seemed quite raving mad, and had no
power over their words and actions. We do not
know the exact form which the affliction took in the
case of this poor girl. It must have been a piteous
sight for her poor mother to see her darling child
under the power of an evil spirit, screaming out and
tearing herself, dashing herself to the ground, and
foaming at the mouth. You know when there is an
afflicted child in a family, the mother's heart seems
drawn more strongly to that poor little one from its
very helplessness and suffering. Whether the child be
deformed in body, crippled, deaf and dumb, or wanting the clear light of reason, the loving mother spares
herself no trouble to amuse and comfort it and lighten
its burden. And brothers and sisters will give up
their own favourite toys and games to amuse the
poor little sufferer. In short it is usually the spoiled
one and pet of the whole family. No doubt it was so
in the case of this poor afflicted little maid. With an
aching heart the fond mother watched over the sufferer and devoted herself to her, ready to give anything, to go anywhere, if she could get any relief for
her darling. At last she heard of JESUS and His
wonderful work in Galilee. How she must have

wished that she was a Jewess, or that JESUS would
come into her country. But there seemed to be no
hope for her. The Jews despised the Gentiles and
called them dogs. JESUS was a Jew, and if she went to
Him it might not be of any use. But still it *might* be ;
and will not a mother catch at even a " might be"
when a child's health and happiness are at stake? At
last she hears that JESUS is close at hand, very near
her own country. Some of her neighbours, living
about Tyre and Sidon, had been to JESUS, mixing
with the multitudes who flocked about Him, and had
heard Him, and had seen Him cast out unclean
spirits and heal all kinds of diseases. There was
no doubt about His *power*, but *would* He heal her
daughter? Oh, if she could anyhow persuade Him !
She determined to try. Yes, and she determined to
try her *utmost*, and not to give up until she had tried
her *very best*. In fact she seems to have made up her
mind not to give up *at all* until she had got help for
her daughter.

JESUS was walking out with His disciples when the
anxious mother came in sight of them. How she
knew Him I cannot tell, perhaps from the description
of some of her neighbours who had seen JESUS ; perhaps she had herself been among those who had gone
from Phœnicia to see Him, but had not on that occasion been able to get near to Him for the crowd that
pressed upon Him. Perhaps some bystander pointed
Him out to her. As soon as she got near enough to
be heard, she cried out—fancy how her poor heart
was beating !—" Have mercy on me, O LORD, Thou
Son of David ; my daughter is grievously vexed with

a devil." Few words, yet they came from a very full
heart, and they contained (1) an appeal for mercy,
(2) a confession of faith, (3) a piteous tale of suffering. How different from the usual vain repetitions of
the heathen or Gentiles, of whom our LORD had said
"They think that they shall be heard for their much
speaking." I am quite sure that this prayer went
straight to the compassionate heart of JESUS. But
neither by look or word did He show that it did. "He
answered her not a word." Yet she would not despair. Again and again she cried to Him Who, she
had come to believe, alone could help her. Still
JESUS was silent, took no notice, "made as though He
heard her not." At last the apostles spoke for her,
but rather, it would seem, to get rid of her than from
any sympathy with her. They were afraid of a scene
which would attract attention to them when they
knew that their Master wanted to be in quiet and
rest. "Send her away," they pleaded, as much as to
say, Give her what she asks and let her go, "for she
crieth after us." Then JESUS broke silence and said,
no doubt loud enough for the poor woman to hear,
"I am not sent but unto the lost sheep of the house
of Israel." "Ah," she might have thought, "just
what I feared, He will not take notice of a Gentile
dog like me." But she would not give up yet. Our
LORD and His disciples appear here to have come to
an end of their walk, and to have reached the house
where they were staying. Another moment and perhaps the door would be shut against her. She ran
forward and threw herself at the feet of JESUS, crying,
"LORD, help me."

The thought of that darkened home, of that darling child's terrible suffering, urged her on. Not for silence, not for cold looks and words could she turn back, with that wan face, those hollow glaring eyes, those screams of fear and suffering, haunting her. "LORD, help me;" what a depth of feeling and earnestness is wrapped up in those three little words! Look at her waiting for the answer of JESUS to her cry, lying before Him, holding His feet or the hem of His robe, gazing up into His face to read her answer there. Perhaps she saw something in His look to give her hope, even when those chilling words fell upon her ear, "It is not meet to take the children's bread and to cast it to dogs." Perhaps the look on His face was kinder than those harsh-sounding words. Certainly He who meant all the while to grant her prayer strengthened her inwardly by His grace and encouraged her to persevere. With wonderful courage and faith she caught at His words. "Truth, LORD, yet the dogs eat of the crumbs which fall from their master's table." As much as to say, "Yea, LORD, Thou sayest true ; it is not right to *take* the children's *bread* and *give* it to the dogs ; *for* the dogs eat of the *crumbs* that *fall* from their master's table. Let me, therefore, not have bread, but only *crumbs :* and do not *give* me even *them*, but let me pick up those that *fall ; for* this is *our* (the dogs') lot." Luther on these words exclaims, "Was not that a master-stroke? She snares CHRIST in His own words." *Now* JESUS gives way. He would not try her any further. He had only *seemed* to be unkind that He might draw out her faith. Who can paint the joy of that mother's heart when instead of rebuking her boldness, JESUS said, " O woman, great is thy faith : be it unto thee even as thou wilt." Fancy her hastening home and finding her darling daughter lying peacefully upon her bed sound in mind and body ! We never hear of that mother and daughter again, but I feel sure that JESUS was never forgotten in that now happy home, and that not an eye in that house was dry when soon afterwards they heard that JESUS had been put to a cruel death upon the cross.

And now what may a Christian child learn from this touching and beautiful story? Surely the power of earnest, persevering prayer. I am afraid that many children " say their prayers" merely as a habit and a duty, going through a familiar form of words night and morning, without thinking of the meaning of the words they use, or really wanting what their lips ask. Is it not so ? Ah, dear children, GOD looks for something more than words. He looks right down into your hearts to see if you really *mean* the words you say. Suppose you were to ask father or mother for something while all the time you were speaking your thoughts were wandering far away, and it was easy to see that you did not much care whether they did what you asked or no. And yet is not this very much what you do when you pray to GOD? Can you expect Him to answer such prayers as these? But if any little child is trying hard to be good and to love JESUS, or struggling to overcome some sinful temper or habit, then if that little child cries out from its heart, " LORD, help me," it will not cry in vain. Sooner or later help *will* come. Sometimes GOD *seems* not to hear our prayers at first, although they do come from our hearts; but it is only to try us. If we are really in earnest, as that poor mother was, GOD *does* hear, and *will* help. You know some people, even those that love you best, do not like to be "bothered" by your keeping on asking again and again for the same thing; but GOD is not like that, He loves us to keep on asking; we cannot "bother" Him. If what we ask is for our real good He is sure to grant it in time. If we soon give up, GOD sees that we are not in earnest, or have no faith in His Love. And remember, this poor woman was pleading not so much for herself as for another. So if we are not selfish in our prayers, if we pray just as earnestly for other as for ourselves, GOD is sure to hear us and help those whom we ask Him to help. I have sometimes seen with pain little children teasing and laughing at a poor child deformed or afflicted in mind. It is thoughtlessness, no doubt, but such thoughtlessness is cruel and wicked. Rather, children should learn to pray for others who have not the health and strength and soundness of mind which they themselves enjoy, should pity them and try to comfort them and make them happy.

Dear children, we can't do much to help ourselves in trouble and temptation, we can't do much to help others that sadly want help, but we can always go in prayer to One Who can and will help those that are in themselves helpless. We need not say many words, only let us mean what we say, and let the cry go up to GOD from our hearts, "LORD, help me."

XXII.

THE GREAT CREDITOR.

" The creditor is come."—2 Kings iv. 1.

A CREDITOR is a person to whom you owe money. "The creditor is come" is no bad news to a person who has got plenty of money. You pay him what you owe, and he goes away, and there is an end of it. But suppose you have no money? Then "the creditor is come" is bad news indeed. Suppose father has been ill or out of work, and by-and-by a man comes round to collect the rents, and he comes to your cottage, and there is no money to pay the rent. He says, "If you don't pay your rent, you must be turned out." He is a hard man, and will take no excuse. "Pay me what thou owest," and if not, your furniture shall be seized, and you and your little ones must be turned out into the street! There is terrible trouble in that house. Well, once there was a poor widow woman who had two sons. Her husband was a good man, and a prophet; but he was poor, and had died and left her in debt. She sold or pawned all that she had, and at last she had nothing left in the house but a pot of oil. The creditor came, and, finding that she had no money to pay him and no furniture worth seizing, he said that he must take her two sons as slaves. In that country this might be done in those days. In this country and in these days of course it could not be done. The poor widow was in great distress. She went to a famous prophet who had known her husband when he was alive, and told him of her trouble; just as, I find, poor people come naturally to their clergyman as their best friend in their hour of need. The prophet asked her what she had got in the house; and when she told him that she had only a pot of oil, he told her to go and borrow of her neighbours a number of empty vessels, and to borrow not a few. Then she was to shut the door upon herself and her two sons, and to pour the oil into all the vessels that she had been able to borrow, and to set aside those which were full. This was a trial of the poor widow's faith, for how could she fill any number of empty vessels out of one pot of oil? Then there is a saying which is often true, "He that goes a borrowing goes a sorrowing." How was it likely that her neighbours would lend her their pots and jars and basins? But she did as she was bidden. The poor are generally very kind to one another, and the widow soon got a good many. She shut the door and began pouring out the oil, while her sons brought the empty vessels to her, and the oil flowed on and on until all the vessels were full, and she called out to her sons to bring another vessel, but they had got no more, and then, and not till then, the oil ceased running. Fancy how surprised the widow and her sons must have been! She hastened to tell the good prophet of her good fortune, and he told her to go and sell the oil and pay her debt, and that she and her sons could live on what remained. No doubt after the creditor was paid they had plenty left. No doubt the oil was good, even the very best, just as when our LORD at Cana, in Galilee, turned water into wine, it was the very best wine. And there was plenty;

if she had had more vessels to fill, they would all have been filled, the oil did not stop so long as there were vessels for it to run into. The prophet did not tell her how many vessels to borrow. He left that to her, just as the same prophet afterwards told the King of Israel to take the arrows and strike upon the ground, he did not say how often. The king struck three times, and stopped. If he had struck oftener he might have beaten the Syrians in battle after battle till he had destroyed them. But whether from laziness or want of faith, he stopped at three times, and so only gained three victories over the Syrians. If the widow had through laziness or want of faith borrowed only three vessels, how vexed she would have been. She would have lost the chance of paying her creditor, and I don't suppose she would have had another chance. But this widow does not seem to have been one of those people who give themselves as little trouble as possible, like Joash, the King of Israel. She must have borrowed a good many vessels, no doubt as many as her neighbours would or could lend her.

We must never think we can do too much to make sure of the salvation of our souls, too much in the service of GOD. S. Peter tells us to give diligence to make our calling and election sure, that is, to take all possible pains about it. Some people seem to think how little pains need they take in GOD's service, how near they dare run to danger. And that reminds me of a story of a lady who wanted to engage a coachman. Three came after the situation. All said they could drive well. She asked the first how near he thought he could drive to the edge of a precipice, and not fall over. He said, within a foot or so. The next said, within half a foot. But the third said, I would keep as far away from it as I possibly could. The lady wisely chose this last. And so, surely, it is the greatest folly for those who have a soul to be saved or lost, to see how near they can go to the edge of the bottom-less pit, and yet just steer clear of it; how near they can go to temptation, and yet just stop short of the act of sin! Do not you be so foolish, dear children; rather think how precious your souls are in the sight of JESUS, and do not think you can be too watchful against sin. Rather remember how JESUS gave Him-self without stint for you, left *all* the riches of heaven, shed all His life-blood for you, and do not think you can ever do too much for Him.

But think again of the text, "The creditor is come." You and I, my children, are in debt. We owe a debt that we can never repay. And who is our creditor? —GOD. And what are our debts?—Our sins. In the LORD's Prayer we say, "Forgive us our trespasses." Now, if you look in the 6th chapter of S. Matthew, you will find that it is there, "Forgive us our debts." And in the 11th chapter of S. Luke it is, "Forgive us our sins, for we also forgive every one that is indebted to us." So sin is called a debt owed to Almighty GOD.

And if you think how often you have been naughty, how many times you have been idle, or greedy, or selfish, or passionate, or untruthful; how many sins of thought, word and deed even little children commit, you will see that the debt you owe to Almighty GOD is a very large one, larger than you can ever repay, for you can never undo or unsay a wrong thing that you

have once done or said. What are you to do before
the creditor comes and orders you to be sold, and
all that you have, and payment to be made? This
Creditor cannot be bought off with vessels of oil or
with gold and silver.

What did Balak say? "Wherewith shall I come
before the LORD, and bow myself before the high
GOD?" "Will the LORD be pleased with thousands
of rams, or with ten thousands of rivers of oil? shall
I give my firstborn for my transgression, the fruit of
my body for the sin of my soul?" (Micah vi. 6, 7).
S. Peter gives the best answer; he says, "Ye know
that ye were not redeemed with corruptible things, as
silver and gold . . . but with the precious Blood of
CHRIST."

Yes, CHRIST has paid the debt for us, and the
Creditor, GOD the FATHER, is satisfied. We have
nothing else to plead, nothing else to offer; GOD will
take nothing else at our hands, but the precious Blood
of CHRIST. For His sake, because of His Blood shed
for us upon the cross, GOD hears us when we pray,
forgive us our sins, our debts. GOD is not a hard
creditor. He wants to let us off our debt, to forgive
us all our sins. Freely and at once He pardons His
children when they say from their hearts "for JESUS'
sake," and plead the precious Blood. Of ourselves we
have nothing, "there is no health in us," no poor widow
more poor or more helpless. Yet we have our pot of
oil, the grace of GOD the HOLY GHOST. But that is
not our own. It is the gift of GOD given to us at our
Baptism. And that grace will never fail us, so long
as we will use it; it will flow on and on and fill our

hearts and flow over into the hearts of others whom we try to help on the way of salvation. It will flow on if we do not check it by our laziness or want of faith, and the love of GOD will be shed in our hearts by the HOLY GHOST which is given unto us, and enable us at least to pay to GOD in some measure, more and more through all eternity, the great debt of gratitude which we owe to Him for all His Fatherly love and goodness to us sinners.

XXIII.

NEMESIS.

" Behold, ye have sinned against the Lord: and be sure your sin will find you out."—Numbers xxxii. 23.

THESE words are often misunderstood. They do not mean that every sin will be sure to be found out. They say nothing of the kind. They say you may be sure your sin will find *you* out. Let us see what gave rise to these words being spoken. The forty years' wandering of the twelve tribes of Israel in the wilderness was now drawing to an end, and they were about to cross over Jordan to take possession of the land promised to their forefathers—to Abraham, Isaac, and Jacob—the land of Canaan. But the two tribes of Gad and Reuben "had a very great multitude of cattle," and seeing that the land on this side Jordan which they had taken from the Amorites and others was suitable for cattle, they wished to settle there, and not to cross over Jordan, and they asked Moses to give them this land as their portion. Moses was at first very angry with them, and insisted upon their going with the rest over Jordan, to help their brethren in their battles against the inhabitants of the land. The Reubenites and Gadites at length promised Moses that they would do so, and that, meanwhile, they would leave their wives and little ones and their cattle behind, and afterwards they would return and dwell in the land. To this proposal Moses consented, and added this warning, " But if ye will not do so, behold, ye have sinned against the LORD : and be sure your sin will find you out." It was a solemn warning, and ·much needed, for experience had taught Moses that they were a fickle, changeable people, whose promises were not to be trusted. So he warns them that, although he would be dead and gone long before it could be seen whether they would do as they had undertaken, yet their sin, if they broke faith with him, would be sure to find them out. The fact is, sin is its own avenger, and brings after it, sooner or later, sure punishment. It may never *be* found out by man, but it will surely find out the sinner. There have been known cases of crimes committed, the doers of which have never been found out, or even suspected. They have borne about with them for years the burden of a secret fault, until at last they have been driven to confess it and give themselves up to justice, feeling that they must deliver themselves of the burden at any cost, or go mad. There are sins of youth which, when perhaps long forgotten, find people out in later years with a terrible retribution. What a striking instance of this we have in the story of Esau ! Esau had despised his birthright in his youth, and sold it to Jacob for a mess of pottage. Forty-five years had passed away, and that act of contempt for GOD's promise, that passing indulgence of his fleshly appetite, had seemingly been entirely forgotten by him. He clearly looked to receiving his father's blessing which conveyed the birthright, as a matter of course. Oh, how bitter his anguish when after all those years his sin had found him out ! "He cried with a great and exceeding bitter cry, and said unto his father, Bless me, even me also, O my father !"

Again, the widow of Zarephath, to whom Elijah was sent, had a son who fell sick and died. This brought back to her memory some great and unknown sin of years long past, "and she said unto Elijah, What have I to do with thee, O thou man of GOD ? art thou come unto me to call my sin to remembrance, and to slay my son ?"

There is a similar expression to the text in Psalm cxl. which conveys a terrible picture to the mind : "Evil shall hunt the wicked person to overthrow him." By GOD's appointment six cities were set apart as cities of refuge—three on one side of the river Jordan, and three on the other—that if any man killed another by accident, he might flee to one of the cities, and be safe there from the Avenger of blood until the death of the high-priest ; but if the Avenger of blood overtook him before he reached the city of refuge, he might kill him. Now, fancy such a pursuit—the Avenger of blood hunting the flying man, eager to take his life for the life which he had destroyed. The city of refuge

is yet far off, the hunted man is straining every muscle
and sinew in his body to reach it in time. He hears
the quick footsteps of the Avenger of blood behind
him, gaining on him step by step. He clenches his
hands in his agony of terror, the sweat stands out in
great drops upon his brow, his eyeballs are almost
starting from their sockets, his tongue cleaves to the
roof of his mouth, and his heart—how it throbs and
palpitates as, gasping for breath, faint and exhausted,
and yet goaded on by fear, he struggles to reach the
goal! I say, imagine this, and you have an image of
a conscience-stricken sinner, goaded on by the stings
of remorse, flying from his sin, that secret sin which is
hunting him down to his doom which he would fain
fly from, but cannot; which he would, but cannot,
forget ; which he would shut his eyes to, but it haunts
him yet, and will give him no rest, no rest.

Ah, my children, sometimes a great trouble, a great
loss, a great suffering, comes upon a man or woman
in after-life, and they know it not, but it is their sin,
the sin of long long ago finding them out. It does
not make this the less true, that few recognise in that
chastisement the Avenger of blood that has been so
long, so surely, hunting them down. Well is it, where
the affliction is felt and recognised as a just retribu
tion, and the long-forgotten and unrepented sin is
brought to their remembrance in the time of adversity,
and is then repented of and confessed while it is not
yet too late! Well might David, looking back into
the past with a dread of the pursuing sin, cry to God,
" O remember not the sins and offences of my youth !"

But there is another way in which you may "be

sure your sin will find you out." If you have lived for any part of your life in a habit of sin, especially of , certain kinds of sin, should you afterwards by the mercy of GOD be led to repentance and earnest seeking to lead a new life, *then* your sin will find you out. It will find you out by throwing numberless difficulties in your way. Memories of evil past will haunt and distress you, memories of things in which you once delighted, but which now are hateful to you; but you cannot forget them, they vex and torment you continually. Evil thoughts assault and hurt your soul, impure, profane jests, oaths and blasphemies which once your tongue poured out like water. They come into your mind at your prayers, at Holy Communion, they seem whispered in your ear at the most solemn times, in the most sacred places. You are reaping as you once sowed; you are tossing restlessly upon the bed that you made so uneasy for yourself to lie upon. You must not complain because your sin has found you out. If you sin, you must not expect it to be just the same with you as if you had never strayed from the paths of purity and innocence.

Then, oh, my children, be warned in time. Avoid sin. Flee from it as from a serpent. Sow not upon the furrows of unrighteousness, and thou shalt not reap them sevenfold. Lay not up for yourselves bitter pangs of self-reproach for your later years. Think, oh, pause and think, when you are tempted to sin, of these warning words, " Be sure your sin will find you out." The less you indulge evil thoughts now, the less they will assault and hurt your soul in after-life. The less you neglect prayer now, the less you will suffer from wandering thoughts in later years. The less far you venture down the hill now, the less hard climbing you will prepare for yourself by-and-by. Seek the LORD early, and you shall find Him easily. And if you have even thus early formed any sinful habit, if at any time you should fall into any sin, do not try to forget, do not try to excuse, do not try to hide it. Remember it with tears of penitence, confess it with a broken and contrite heart. Find out your sins now, to repent and forsake them, and ask pardon for the dear sake of Him Who died for you; find out your sins thus now, and they will not find *you* out in the great day.

JESUS is our only Refuge from sin. There is no safety from the Avenger of blood but at the foot of His cross, no hiding-place from pursuing evil but by His wounded side. His pierced hands are stretched out to save all who come to Him, and no evil can touch those who place themselves under His mighty protection. But if you harden your hearts and blindly follow your own lusts and desires, unrepentant, un-forgiven, "be sure that your sin will find you out," oh! how terribly, in that great day.

XXIV.

THE BRAVE SHEPHERD-BOY.

" Thy servant slew both the lion and the bear."—1 Samuel xvii. 36.

In the days of King Saul there lived at Bethlehem in Judæa an old man named Jesse, who had eight sons. The youngest was a lad named David, whose business it was to look after his father's sheep. We hear of him for the first time upon the occasion of the visit of Samuel to Bethlehem. Samuel came by GOD's command to anoint one of Jesse's sons to be King of Israel in the room of Saul. Samuel did not know which of Jesse's sons he was to anoint, and when Eliab, the eldest, stood before him, Samuel saw that he was such a fine-looking man that he thought this must be the one whom he was to anoint, but GOD told Samuel that he was mistaken, and that he should not judge by outward appearances.

GOD saw Eliab's heart, his real character, and refused him. One after another the seven elder sons passed before Samuel, but GOD chose none of them. Then Samuel asked Jesse if all his sons were there. Jesse said, " There remaineth yet the youngest, and behold he keepeth the sheep." Samuel told Jesse to send and fetch him. So the young shepherd-boy, who was probably thinking of nothing less than being a king, came and stood before Samuel. Fancy David's surprise when the messengers came to him

and told him that the great prophet had sent for him!
What can he want with me, a poor little shepherd
boy? David must have thought. His father had not
thought it worth while to take little David with him
when he went with the rest of his sons to meet
Samuel. And perhaps poor little David had looked
with a wistful eye after his brothers as they marched
proudly off with their father, and wished he might go
too and see the famous prophet.

And now it turned out after all that poor despised
David was the very one whom the prophet wished to
see. What could it all mean? And when he came,
Samuel took him and poured the anointing oil upon
his head, pointing him out as the future King of
Israel, of GOD's chosen people. More wonderful
still! And from that day the Spirit of the LORD
came upon David. What must have been the thoughts
of that shepherd-boy as he sat on the hill-side watching his father's sheep, as more than one thousand
years after, other shepherds were watching their sheep
in the same spot, when an angel came from heaven to
tell them that to them was born that day in the city
of David a SAVIOUR, CHRIST the LORD! How he
must have thought, again and again, of the events of
that memorable day, and wondered when and how it
should come to pass that he should be king!

Well, time passed on, and after a while messengers
came again for David, the shepherd-boy. This time
they came to fetch him to court. As he sat watching
the sheep, he used to pass away the time by compos-
ing and singing psalms, and accompanying himself on
the harp, which he had learned to play beautifully.

No doubt it was then he sang the twenty-third Psalm,
"The LORD is my Shepherd" . . . . . . "Thou
anointest my head with oil." And when he came to
the court of King Saul, and soothed with the sweet
strains of his harp the troubled soul of the king in
his fits of madness, very likely he thought that now
the promise was soon to be fulfilled that he himself
should be king. But he had many years to wait yet
and much trouble and danger to go through first.

After a time the Philistines came to fight against
Israel, and David was sent back again from court to
feed the sheep as before. And then it may have been
that while David was watching the sheep, there came
at one time a fierce lion, and at another time a bear,
and tried to carry off the lambs of David's little flock,
and David, trusting in GOD, bravely went after the
lion and bear, and killed both of them. So when,
by-and-by, Jesse sent David to take some food to his
three eldest brothers, who were soldiers in King Saul's
army, and David wanted to go and fight Goliath, the
Philistine giant, whom everybody else was afraid of,
David told the King that by GOD's help he had been
able to kill those two wild beasts, and so he did not
doubt that GOD would enable him to kill the giant
also. And so you know he did, and cut off his head
with Goliath's own sword, and gained a great victory
for Israel. It was a great thing to kill a lion and a
bear, but it was a still greater thing to kill an armed
giant eleven feet high, whom all those brave, strong
soldiers were afraid of.

Now in all this, David was a type of CHRIST, the
Anointed One, Who laid down His life for the sheep,

and fought him of whom Goliath was a type, the
Devil, and destroyed his power, and gained a great
victory for us all. And we too must go forth, like
David, trusting in the LORD, to fight against that great
enemy of GOD's people, the Devil. And as David
could not go against the Philistine in the armour
which Saul gave him, but with the simple weapons
which GOD taught him to use, we cannot overcome
the Devil by human means, or in our own strength,
"the weapons of our warfare are not carnal," but we
must overcome him by faith and by the simple weapons
of the Gospel, the Sacraments, and other means of
grace which our blessed LORD, the Captain of our
Salvation, puts into our hands.

Again, as David fought and killed the lion and the
bear before he slew Goliath, so you, my children,
must overcome the smaller sins which tempt children,
that you may have confidence and strength to fight
against the stronger temptations that will beset you in
after life, as you grow up to manhood and woman-
hood. If you run away from lions and bears now,
you will run away from giants by-and-by. If you
smite the lions and bears in childhood, you will go
forth brave and strong in faith against Goliaths in
after years. "He that is faithful in that which is least
is faithful also in much." If we would gain strength
and courage to resist when a great temptation comes
upon us, we must be watchful and faithful in resisting
the little daily and hourly temptations. And it is a
great thing to learn to resist the beginnings of evil.
Many a temptation which is at first but, as it were, a
lion or a bear, will become a great giant if we do not

hasten to smile it at once. It is easier, when you are
first tempted to anger, to keep your temper; but if
once you let your temper get the better of you, you
will find it a very giant in strength. You know, in
your games, if you are always beaten by another, you
lose heart, and if in childhood you are always giving
way to temptation, you will have no heart to resist in
youth and riper age. But if, by the grace of GOD,
you now make a bold stand against sin and overcome
it, you will have the remembrance of GOD's help in
former fights to encourage you hereafter. You will
feel "the LORD that delivered me out of the paw of
the lion, and out of the paw of the bear, He will
deliver me out of the hand of this Philistine."

Be watchful and brave, children, and do your duty
faithfully, trusting in the LORD, and however humble
be the station of life to which it has pleased GOD to
call you, He Who took David from the sheepfolds
and made him a king, will in due time call you to
His court and set you among the princes of His
people. You have CHRIST's own word for it, "To
him that overcometh will I grant to sit with Me in
My throne, even as I also overcame, and am set
down with My FATHER in His throne."

XXV.

THE WRESTLERS.

*" For we wrestle not against flesh and blood, but against princi-
palities, against powers, against the rulers of the darkness of this
world, against spiritual wickedness in high places."*—Ephesians
vi. 12.

ON a large plain there were assembled a great number of people separated into two parties wrestling
together. The plain was bounded on one side by a
deep gulf or abyss, towards which one set of combatants was trying to drag the other. On the other
side, the plain was bounded by a narrow stream, which
divided it from a most beautiful and fertile land. I
will not tell you that I saw this in a dream, because
that would not be true; but I seemed to see it brought
before my mind's eye while I was meditating upon the
passage of GOD's Word which heads this sermon. I
seemed to draw nearer to look at these wrestlers.
Some I saw being dragged almost unresistingly towards
the abyss. They were making little or no effort to
save themselves, and could not be said to be wrestling
at all. Even on the brink of that fearful gulf they
seemed quite unaware of their danger, and smilingly
assured their friends, as they were hurried along, that
they were quite happy. With these poor idiots, for I
can call them nothing else, I had no concern, my
attention was soon fixed on a pair of real wrestlers.
One was a fine, active-looking young man, with bright
eyes and a fair complexion. Confident of victory, he
eyed his foe with a scornful air of superiority. He

would not have been so scornful and confident if he had seen his enemy as I saw him; for a more hideous and terrible-looking being I never beheld, and there was a cruel glitter in his evil eye which made me shudder to see. But something whispered to me that the youth and most others of his party could not see their foes as they really were; and the nearer they were dragged to the edge of the abyss, the less clearly did they see the real forms of those who dragged them thither, while the nearer they got to the beautiful land of light which lay across the stream, the more plainly they saw the hateful features of their foes.

But, as I gazed, a bright ray of light from the beautiful land fell for a moment on the form of him who wrestled with the youth, and the young man's look became more grave, and he knit his brow and set his teeth, and, grasping his enemy more firmly, he put forth all his strength in a great effort to throw him off, and escape towards that fair land. Now came the tug of war, foot to foot, eye watching eye, they wrestled till the sweat poured down the youth's face, and the muscles stood out upon his strong arms and sturdy back and hips as though they would burst the skin. His enemy, too, strained every nerve to throw him, tried every art and trick such as practised wrestlers know, but in vain, for I saw a Mighty One standing by the youth, who held him up, and would not let him fall. But now I saw that the evil-eyed one had confederates, who were trying by all kinds of arts to catch the young man's eye, and draw his attention off from his foe. Some played soft music, others shouted and sang, others held up glittering jewels, crowns and

sceptres, while others changed themselves into shapes
of seeming beauty which smiled and beckoned to him,
and, ah ! before long, the youth, weary of the struggle,
let his eye dwell longingly on one of these, and in a
moment he was down—a grievous fall, but, raised up
again by that Mighty One, he renewed the struggle
until, off his guard once more, he was thrown again,
and again and again after that, and each fall left him
weaker ; and nearer and nearer, while he was down,
the enemy dragged him towards the precipice.   It was
a sickening sight, and I would gladly have turned
away to watch a more successful wrestler, but a strange
fascination held me to the spot, and I could not choose
but watch the end, which was now drawing terribly
near.

Yes, only a few feet now from the edge of that awful
chasm !   The foe looked triumphant, the young man
seemed quite unconscious of his peril, and was now
dragged almost unresistingly along, until suddenly
there came a loud peal of thunder, and a vivid flash
of lightning showed him through the darkness which
had grown around him his terrible danger.   With a
loud cry of terror he struggled with fierce energy
against his dread adversary; but the footing was
treacherous and slippery now, and frequent falls had
exhausted his strength, and the cruel foe seemed to
despise his puny efforts, and still dragged him slowly
but surely to his doom.   Was there no hope ?   Yes, if
he would cry to that Mighty One who stood, I saw,
still within call, he might be rescued even now.   But
would he ? did he ?   I cannot tell ; for there came
another burst of thunder sound, and in the flash that

followed I saw them struggling on the very brink, and then—all was hidden from my eyes. Only I heard a fearful cry of despair which pierced my inmost soul; but whether it came from the youth falling into that dreadful gulf, or from the enemy robbed of his prey when he had thought it secure, I may not know.

I turned to seek another pair of combatants; and lo! I saw a little child struggling bravely with one of those terrible beings. It could not have stood for a moment, you would have thought; yet in truth it did stand most manfully, and gave its great strong enemy many a heavy fall, while the child fell but seldom, and that very lightly, and was up again directly, and every time the enemy was thrown the little fellow set off running towards the beautiful land across the stream. The child made little account of the glittering toys and sparkling cups and beckoning shapes that had so beguiled the youth whom I had lately watched, and whenever he turned his eyes away from his foe, it was but to look, now pleadingly, now gratefully, on the kind, cheering Face of the Mighty One who stood near him, and gave him strength to wrestle with the enemy.

It was dreadful to see the rage of that enemy when he got a fall, and found that his strength could not avail to overthrow his childish antagonist. Often indeed he pressed him hard and got him down upon his knees, but at such times the child only seemed to gather fresh strength as soon as his knees touched the ground. So the strife went on, and nearer and nearer the child drew to the narrow stream until, at last, with one great effort he threw the dark foe far from him, and holding the hand of his mighty Friend, plunged

into the waters, and, as he went, I heard him say, " I
have fought a good fight, I have finished my course, I
have kept the faith; henceforth there is laid up for me
a crown of righteousness ;" and softly as a peal of
bells across the water came to my ears the sound of
angel-voices singing, "Out of the mouths of babes
and sucklings hast Thou ordained strength, because of
Thine enemies, that Thou mightest still the enemy
and the avenger."

Now, dear children, I think you will easily have
understood that the "plain" is this life, the narrow
stream is the death of the righteous through which
they pass to the beautiful land of Heaven beyond.
The fearful gulf is the death of the wicked through
which they fall into the bottomless pit of hell-fire.
The wrestlers are men and evil spirits. Those who
wrestle not at all, but suffer themselves to be led unresistingly to destruction are the careless, thoughtless
sinners who make no attempt to resist temptation,
and die self-deceived, saying, "Peace, peace, when
there is no peace." The young man who wrestled,
but so unsuccessfully, is a type of those who strive
against sin, but trust to their own strength, instead of
looking to CHRIST, and depending entirely on Him
for victory. The confederates of the foe are those
allies of the devil, the world and the flesh, with their
deceptive pleasures. The thunder and lightning are
the last warning mercifully given by GOD, a last call
in the terror of approaching death, when, if the sinner
will yet turn to his SAVIOUR, he may even at the last
hour be delivered from eternal death. The little child
is a type of those who, like you, are yet children in

years, as well as of those who, having ceased to be children in years, are yet children in heart, leaning with childlike trustfulness on Him Who is mighty to save. They, driven by strong temptation to fall on their knees in prayer, only gain more strength for the fight, and though they may sometimes fall into sin, as who does not? yet they fall not into great and deadly sins, and quickly rise again, made humble, but not despondent, by the fall.

See, then, dear children, what a real, earnest struggle each of us must go through if we would gain the crown of victory at last! We can do nothing without trouble, gain nothing without toil. It is a great blessing to be able to read and write and to gain knowledge; but to do this, lessons must be learned, playhours shortened, and much hard work gone through. And the more worth having anything is, even in this world, the more pains must we take to win it. Well, then, we cannot expect to get that which is so much more worth having than anything on earth, namely, everlasting happiness in Heaven, without taking a great deal of trouble, and giving up much pleasure for the sake of it.

We must not expect to get Heaven easily, when we cannot get anything great and good, even here, easily. And if S. Paul had to wrestle, for he says "*we* wrestle," surely we cannot expect to go where he has gone without wrestling too. No, we must all *wrestle*. But our enemies are not flesh-and-blood enemies, but evil spirits, mighty powers, rulers of darkness, unseen enemies, and so all the more terrible. We cannot beat them in our own strength; a worm might as well try to conquer a mighty eagle; but if we wrestle,

JESUS will help us, and we shall be sure to win. The
weakest child, with JESUS on his side, is stronger than
all the bad spirits in hell. Then it will be indeed
"Resist the devil, and he," for all his strength and
cunning "will flee from you."

You cannot, as I said, *see* these evil spirits ; but you
can always tell when they are near, and are trying to
make you fall. When you feel too idle to attend to
your lessons, when you feel peevish or discontented,
or cross and angry, when you do not want to say your
prayers or to go to church, or to give up your own
way, when you are tempted to be greedy or conceited,
vain of your new clothes, or of your cleverness, or of
anything else, then be sure that your enemy is putting
forth his strength to make you fall, and draw you
farther away from Heaven ; then is the time to wrestle,
and pray to JESUS for help. And always you need to
be watchful lest these enemies come upon you un-
awares, and give you a sad fall. And if you should
thus fall at any time, make haste to rise again by
owning your fault and asking forgiveness from GOD,
resolving to be more watchful in time to come. It is
hard work, very hard while it lasts, all this wrestling
against sin ; but it is only for a little while, and then
comes rest for those who have toiled, a crown for those
who have fought, a beautiful crown from the LORD's
hand ; for those who have denied themselves, giving
up little pleasures here, there is fulness of joy in the
Presence of JESUS, and at GOD's right hand pleasures
for evermore.

May you, dear children, wrestle bravely, and GOD
give you the victory, through JESUS CHRIST our LORD.

"There is a land of pure delight,
    Where saints immortal reign ;
Infinite day excludes the night,
    And pleasures banish pain.

"There everlasting spring abides,
    And never-withering flowers :
Death, like a narrow sea, divides
    This heavenly land from ours.

"Sweet fields beyond the swelling flood
    Stand dressed in living green ;
So to the Jews old Canaan stood
    While Jordan rolled between.

"But timorous mortals start and shrink
    To cross this narrow sea,
And linger, shivering on the brink,
    And fear to launch away.

"O could we make our doubts remove,
    Those gloomy doubts that rise ;
And see the Canaan that we love,
    With unbeclouded eyes ;

"Could we but stand where Moses stood,
    And view the landscape o'er,
Not Jordan's stream, nor death's cold flood,
    Should fright us from the shore."

XXVI.

FORGETFULNESS OF GOD.

" If we have forgotten the name of our God, or stretched out our hands to a strange god : shall not God search this out ? for He knoweth the secrets of the heart."—Psalm xliv. 20, 21.

A FATHER once sent forth two of his children to do something for him. One was bidden to go and take some message to a poor sick woman, the other was told to go and sweep out a certain room. Neither of the children were told how far they would have to go, but each had sufficient directions given him to enable him to find the house to which he was sent. Their Father told them that they must attend carefully to his directions, for otherwise they would most likely lose the way. And he warned them that they would meet with many difficulties and dangers, which he showed them how to avoid ; and he gave them, moreover, many helps to keep their errand in remembrance, and to pass safely through the dangers and hardships of the way. So he sent them forth. Now the one of these children who was sent to take the message to the poor sick woman, before he had gone far, met with a number of other children who persuaded him to play with them at various games, and to go to a fair and see one wonderful sight or show after another. He did not like to tell them that his Father had sent him with a message to an old sick woman, for fear they should laugh at him and his

Father too, and he thought he should have plenty of time, after amusing himself awhile, to find out the sick woman and do his errand. But he became so taken up with his companions and their droll ways and pleasant amusements, that after a bit he quite forgot all about his Father, and the work he had to do, and did not notice how the time was passing, until at last a very grave-looking person came up to him and he saw that it was one of his Father's servants, and then he remembered about the poor old woman, and felt quite frightened to think how the time had slipped away, and he cried out, " Wait a bit, don't take me back to Father yet, he will be so angry, there will be just time for me to run and give his message first." But the servant did not seem to hear a word that he said, he only caught hold of him with his hand, and oh ! such a cold hand, and carried him straight off to his Father.

Now before I tell you what his Father said to him, I will tell you about the other son. He too, I am sorry to say, forgot all about his Father's errand. He too met with some companions, and they asked him where he was going. When he told them, they laughed, and said, "Come with us and we will show you a much more profitable way of spending your time and strength than that, that is too menial a task for a fine boy like you." And then they showed him some gold dust, and bright sparkling diamonds, and said, " Come along, we will all have one purse." And the boy remembered that his Father had said, " My son, when sinners entice thee, consent thou not." But he looked at the gold, and thought, Well, there

can be no harm in just going for a little while, and I
can spend what I get in buying some nice gift for my
Father, and then I shall still have time to sweep the
room, *that* will not take long. So he went with them
and gathered such a quantity of gold and silver and
precious stones that he quite forgot about the room
he had to sweep, and at last he got so rich, that he
determined to build a beautiful house and enjoy his
wealth, but just then he heard a voice close by which
said, " Thou fool, this night shall thy soul be required
of thee," and in a moment the icy hand of his
Father's servant was laid upon him, and all his riches
turned to ashes, and he had nothing to take to his
Father whose work he had neglected.

And now these two children had to face their angry
Father. They heard his voice, but they dared not
look up, they wished to hide away from him, but they
knew they could not escape. And now he asks the
first why he had not given his message to the poor
woman ? and he stammers out the excuse, " Oh, I
am so sorry, I really forgot, I did indeed ; try me
again, send me once more and I will let nothing stop
me or turn me aside till I have done your errand."
But the Father says, " Too late, my son, too late, the
message was taken, but not by you, and your reward
is given to another." Then the boy lifted up his
voice and cried, " Hast thou not a blessing left for
me ? Bless me too, O my Father." But his Father
said, " Your crown is gone, your place is filled up,
you are disinherited. Go from my sight." And then
his old companions who had enticed him to play,
rushed forward and carried him away with them,

shrieking with fright, for he saw that they meant anything but play *now*.

And then the Father turned to the other son, and he too could only say that he had forgotten what his Father had told him. His work could not be done by another, and he was delivered up to those who had led him astray to be tormented, and condemned to dwell for ever a prisoner in the room he had neglected to sweep.

Now this is a kind of parable. I dare say you have already guessed something of its meaning. The Father is GOD. The two sons represent two different classes of men, the pleasure-seekers and the money-seekers. Whereas one had to sweep out a room, this shows first, that no work is to be thought beneath us that GOD gives us to do ; and secondly, in that no one else could do this work, by the room is meant the soul of man, which he has to sweep clean from all the dirt and rubbish of sin, and prepare it to be a clean and fitting abode for the Presence of GOD.

The grave-looking servant is Death. He is deaf. It is no use asking him to wait. How many people are surprised by death, before they have even begun the work which GOD gives them to do !

And whereas another had attended to the sick woman, GOD gives one man opportunities of doing good, and if he will not do it, GOD's work must be done by some one, He gives the work and its reward to another. "Hold fast that thou hast, that no man take thy crown." But no one else could do the other son's work, because if a man will not prepare his own soul, no one else can do it for him. "No man may redeem his brother, nor make atonement to GOD for him, so he must let that alone for ever." The sinful pleasures and temptations of riches that entice men to forget GOD are evil spirits, who will torment their dupes and victims in hell fire for ever.

The two children met with none of the difficulties and dangers their Father had warned them of, because they had not entered the strait gate nor walked in the narrow way, but had chosen the broad way that leadeth to destruction.

Now I hope that from this story, dear children, you will learn this, never to forget GOD, even in your youth. "Remember *now* thy Creator in the days of thy youth," and that you will learn that GOD has sent you into the world to work for Him.

You have to prepare yourself for the place which JESUS is preparing for you amongst the many mansions of His FATHER'S House. You have your own room to sweep, your own soul to purify. Besides this, you are sent on an errand of mercy to others. Even little children can find some one to help and comfort and to show kindness to for JESUS' sake. Do not neglect your own soul. Do not neglect to do good to others. Use the helps your FATHER in Heaven has given you, His Word and Sacraments, and prayer, and GOD will strengthen you, and will accept all you do for JESUS' sake, and reward you at last far more than you can ever deserve.

J. MASTERS and Co., Printers, Albion Buildings, Bartholomew Close.

A LIST

OF

Theological and Devotional Works

PUBLISHED BY

J. MASTERS AND CO.,

78, NEW BOND STREET, LONDON.

A LIST OF
THEOLOGICAL AND DEVOTIONAL WORKS

PUBLISHED BY

J. MASTERS AND CO.

THE REV. J. M. NEALE, D.D.

A COMMENTARY ON THE PSALMS, from Primitive and Mediæval Writers; and from the various Office Books and Hymns of the Roman, Mozarabic, Ambrosian, Gallican, Greek, Coptic, Armenian, and Syriac Rites. By the late Rev. J. M. NEALE, D.D., and the Rev. R. F. LITTLEDALE, LL.D. Four Vols. Post 8vo., cloth, £2. 2s.

Vol. 1. *Third edition.* Psalm I. to Psalm XXXVIII., with Three Dissertations. 10s. 6d.
Vol. 2. *Second edition.* Psalm XXXIX. to Psalm LXXX. 10s. 6d.
Vol. 3. *Second edition.* Psalm LXXXI. to Psalm CXVIII. 10s. 6d.
Vol. 4. Psalm CXIX. to CL. With Index of twelve thousand Scripture References. 10s. 6d.

SERMONS PREACHED IN SACKVILLE COLLEGE CHAPEL. Four Vols., Crown 8vo.
Vol. 1. Advent to Whitsun Day. Second Edition. 7s. 6d.
Vol. 2. Trinity and Saints' Days. Second Edition. 7s. 6d.
Vol. 3. Lent and Passiontide. 7s. 6d.
Vol. 4. The Minor Festivals of the Church. Third Edition. 6s.

SERMONS PREACHED IN A RELIGIOUS HOUSE. Two Vols., Fcap. 8vo., 10s.

SERMONS PREACHED IN A RELIGIOUS HOUSE. Second Series. Two Vols., Fcap., 8vo. 10s.

HISTORY OF THE HOLY EASTERN CHURCH.—General Introduction. Two Vols., £2.

THE HISTORY OF THE PATRIARCHATE OF ALEXANDRIA. Two Vols., 24s.

SEATONIAN POEMS. Fcap. 8vo., 3s. 6d.

MEDIÆVAL HYMNS, SEQUENCES, AND OTHER POEMS, translated by the Rev. J. M. NEALE. Second Edition. 2s.

HYMNS FOR THE SICK: for the hours, days of the week, &c. 6d., cloth, 1s.

HYMNS FOR CHILDREN. First, Second, and Third Series. 3d. each. Complete in cloth, 1s.

THE REV. T. T. CARTER, M.A.,
Rector of Clewer; Hon. Canon of Christ Church, Oxford.

THE DOCTRINE OF THE PRIESTHOOD IN THE CHURCH OF ENGLAND. Second Edition. 4s.

THE DOCTRINE OF CONFESSION IN THE CHURCH OF ENGLAND. Second Edition. Post 8vo., 6s.

SERMONS. Third Edition. 8vo., 9s.

SPIRITUAL INSTRUCTIONS ON THE HOLY EUCHA-RIST. Crown 8vo. Fourth Edition. 3s. 6d.

SPIRITUAL INSTRUCTIONS ON THE DIVINE REVE-LATIONS. Crown 8vo. 4s.

LENT LECTURES. 8vo., cloth, 8s.

1. The Imitation of our LORD. Fifth Edition. 2s. 6d.
2. The Passion and Temptation of our LORD. Second Edition. 3s.
3. The Life of Sacrifice. Second Edition. 2s. 6d.
4. The Life of Penitence. Second Edition. 2s. 6d.

FAMILY PRAYERS. Third Edition. Cloth, 1s.

THE DOCTRINE OF THE HOLY EUCHARIST, drawn from the Holy Scriptures and the Records of the Church of England. Third Edition. Fcap. 8vo., 9d.

EDITED BY THE REV. T. T. CARTER.

A BOOK OF PRIVATE PRAYER for Morning, Mid-day, Night and other times, with Rules for those who would live to GOD amid the business of daily life. Tenth Edition, limp cloth, 1s.; cloth, red edges, 1s. 3d.; roan, 1s. 6d.; calf, 3s. 6d.

LITANIES AND OTHER DEVOTIONS. 1s. 6d.

MEMORIALS FOR USE IN A RELIGIOUS HOUSE. Second Edition. 6d.

NIGHT OFFICES FOR THE HOLY WEEK. 8vo., 2s. 6d.

THE FOOTPRINTS OF THE LORD ON THE KING'S HIGHWAY OF THE CROSS. Devotional Aids for Holy Week. Fcap. 8vo., cloth, 1s.

FOOTSTEPS OF THE HOLY CHILD, being Readings on the Incarnation. Part I., 1s. Part II., 3s. 6d. In 1 vol. 4s. 6d. cloth.

MANUAL OF DEVOTION FOR SISTERS OF MERCY. In Eight Parts, wrapper; or, Two Vols., cloth, 10s.

SHORT OFFICE OF THE HOLY GHOST. 1s.

THE RIGHT REV. A. P. FORBES, D.C.L.,
Bishop of Brechin.

ARE YOU BEING CONVERTED? Sermons on Serious Subjects. Third Edition. Fcap. 8vo., 2s.

SERMONS ON THE GRACE OF GOD, and other Cognate Subjects. 3s. 6d.

A COMMENTARY ON THE LITANY. Fcap. 8vo., cloth, 3s. 6d.

4   [*J. Masters & Co.,*

A COMMENTARY ON THE TE DEUM, from ancient sources.
2s., cloth; cheap edition, 1s.

A COMMENTARY ON THE CANTICLES USED IN
THE PRAYER BOOK. 2s., cheap edition, 1s.

A COMMENTARY ON THE SEVEN PENITENTIAL
PSALMS, from ancient sources. Cloth, 1s.

THEOLOGICAL DEFENCE for the Bishop of Brechin on a Pre-
sentment by the Rev. W. Henderson and others, on certain points concerning the doctrine of the Holy Eucharist. 8vo., 6s.

A PRIMARY CHARGE DELIVERED TO THE CLERGY
OF HIS DIOCESE. Third edition. 1s.

EDITED BY THE BISHOP OF BRECHIN.

MEDITATIONS ON THE SUFFERING LIFE OF OUR
LORD. Translated from Pinart. Fifth Edition. 5s.; calf antique,
10s.

NOURISHMENT OF THE CHRISTIAN SOUL. Translated
from Pinart. Fourth Edition. 5s.; calf antique, 10s.

MEMORIALE VITÆ SACERDOTALIS; or, Solemn Warnings
of the Great Shepherd, JESUS CHRIST, to the Clergy of His Holy Church.
Translated from the Latin. Second Edition. Fcap. 8vo., 3s. 6d.

MEDITATIONS ON THE PASSION OF OUR LORD
JESUS CHRIST, according to the Four Evangelists, by the Abbot
of Monte Cassino. 18mo., 2s.

THE MIRROR OF YOUNG CHRISTIANS. Translated from
the French. With Engravings, 2s, 6d. Morocco antique, 7s. Cheap
Edition, 1s.

THE RIGHT REV. J. R. WOODFORD, D.D.,
Lord Bishop of Ely.

SERMONS, preached in various Churches of Bristol. Second Edition.
7s. 6d.

OCCASIONAL SERMONS. Vol. I., 7s. 6d. Vol. II., 7s. 6d.

ORDINATION SERMONS, preached in the Dioceses of Oxford and
Winchester, 1860—1872. 8vo., 6s. 6d.

THE RIGHT REV. R. MILMAN, D.D.,
Lord Bishop of Calcutta.

THE LOVE OF THE ATONEMENT; a Devotional Exposition
of the 53rd chapter of Isaiah. Fourth Edition. Fcap. 8vo., cloth, 3s. 6d.

CONVALESCENCE. Thoughts for those who are recovering from
Sickness. Fcap. 8vo., 1s.

THE VOICES OF HARVEST. 8d.; cloth, 1s.

THE WAY THROUGH THE DESERT; or, The Caravan. 6d.;
1s. cloth.

MEDITATIONS ON CONFIRMATION. 3d.

THEOLOGICAL, &c.

ACTS OF THE APOSTLES, The. An Exposition of the leading Events recorded in that Book. Cloth, 1s.

ADAMS, Rev. R.—A Commentary on the Prayer Book, for the use of overworked Pastors and Teachers in the Church and School. Fcp. 8vo. 4s.

ARDEN, Rev. G.—Manual of Catechetical Instruction. 2s.

BAGOT, Mrs. C. W.—Selections from the Letters of S. Francis de Sales. Translated from the French. Revised by a Priest of the English Church. Fourth edition. Fcap. 8vo., cloth, 1s. 6d.

BLACKMORE, Rev. R. W.
The Doctrine of the Russian Church, &c. Translated from the Sclavonic-Russian by the Rev. R. W. Blackmore. 8vo., 4s.
Harmony of Anglican Doctrines with those of the Catholic and Apostolic Church of the East. 8vo., 3s.
History of the Church of Russia, by A. N. Mouravieff. Translated by the Rev. R. W. Blackmore. 8vo., 10s. 6d.

BOOK OF GENESIS, The. An Exposition of the Leading Events recorded in it. Fcap. 8vo., cloth, 1s.

BOOK OF CHURCH HISTORY, founded on the Rev. W. Palmer's "Ecclesiastical History." Fifth edition. 18mo., 1s.

BROWNE, C.—A Lecture on Symbolism and its connection with Church Art, Architecture, &c. Third edition, with 42 Illustrations, and Appendix on the Symbolism of the Ecclesiastical Vestments. 1s. 6d.

BROWN, Rev. R. C. L.—The Life of Peace. Fcap. 8vo.

CATECHISM OF THEOLOGY. 18mo., cloth, 1s. 6d.; wrapper, 1s.

CHAMBERLAIN, Rev. T.—The Epistle to the Romans. With Short Notes chiefly Critical and Doctrinal. Fcap. 8vo., cloth, 2s.

CHAPTERS ON THE TE DEUM. By the Author of "Earth's Many Voices." 16mo., cloth, 2s.

CHRIST IN THE LAW; or, the Gospel Foreshadowed in the Pentateuch. Compiled from various sources. By a Priest of the Church of England. Fcap. 8vo., 3s. 6d.

CHRIST IN THE PROPHETS: Joshua, Judges, Samuel, Kings. Fcap. 8vo., 4s. 6d.

CHRISTIAN SERVANT (The) taught from the Catechism her Faith and Practice. By the Author of the "Servants' Hall." Edited by the Rev. Sir W. H. Cope, Bart. Fcap. 8vo., cloth. (Pub. 7s.) *Reduced to* 3s.

CHURCH DOCTRINES PROVED BY THE BIBLE. Fcap. 8vo., 1s.

COMPANION TO THE SUNDAY SERVICES of the Church of England. 2s. 6d.

DAILY EVENTS OF HOLY WEEK. Written in Plain Words. Fcap. 8vo., 6d.; cloth, 1s.

EASY LESSONS FOR THE YOUNGER CHILDREN IN SUNDAY SCHOOLS. By the Author of "Conversations with Cousin Rachel." 4d.
Questions, for the Use of the Teacher. 6d.

EASY CATECHISM OF THE OLD TESTAMENT HISTORY, with the dates of the principal events. Third edition. 18mo., 3d

ECCLESIOLOGY, Hand-Book of English. Companion for Church Tourists. Cloth, 2s.

EUCHARISTIC MONTH; being short Daily Preparation and Thanksgiving for the Holy Communion. Cloth, 1s.

6   [*J. Masters & Co.,*

FASTS AND FESTIVALS OF THE CHURCH, in a conversational form. 1s. 8d.

FORD, Rev. J.—The Gospels, &c., illustrated from Ancient and Modern Authors. 8vo.

      S. Matthew, 11s.   S. Luke, 12s.

      S. Mark, 11s.   S. John, 12s.

      The Acts of the Apostles, 13s.

      S. Paul's Epistle to the Romans, 12s.

GREAT TRUTHS OF THE CHRISTIAN RELIGION.
Edited by the Rev. W. U. RICHARDS. Fifth edition. 3s. cloth; or in Five Parts, wrappers, 2s. 6d.

GRESLEY, Rev. W.

Thoughts on Religion and Philosophy. Fcap. 8vo. 4s.

Priests and Philosophers. Fcap. 8vo. 3s. 6d.

HEYGATE, Rev. W. E.—Catholic Antidotes. Post 8vo., 5s. 6d.

HOPKINS, Bishop.—The Law of Ritualism, examined in its Relation to the Word of GOD, to the Primitive Church, to the Church of England, and to the Protestant Episcopal Church in the United States. Second edit., 2s. A Reprint of the above, for distribution, in fcap. 8vo., 1s.

HOSMER, Rev. A. H.—Hearing Mass and other Customs considered. 8vo., 2s. 6d.

HOUSMAN, Rev. H.

Readings on the Psalms, with Notes on their Musical Treatment, originally addressed to Choristers. Fcap. 8vo., cloth, 3s. 6d.

Sermon Stories for Children's Services and Home Reading. 16mo., cl., 2s.

HOW TO FOLLOW CHRIST; or, Plain Words about our LORD's Life. By the Author of "Our New Life in CHRIST," &c. Fcap. 8vo., cloth, 6s. 6d., or in 12 Parts.

HOW TO COME TO CHRIST. By the Author of "Our New Life in CHRIST." Fcap. 8vo., 6d.

HUTCHINGS, Rev. W. H.

The Person and Work of the Holy Ghost. A Doctrinal and Devotiona Treatise. Second Edition. Crown 8vo., cloth, 4s.

Some Aspects of the Cross. Second Edition. Crown 8vo., cloth, 4s.

LEA, Rev. W.

Catechisings on the Prayer Book. Third edition. 18mo., cloth, 1s.

Catechisings on the Life of our LORD. 12mo , cloth, 3s. 6d.

LESSONS FOR LITTLE CHILDREN ON THE SEASONS OF THE CHURCH. By C. A. R. 1s.

LESSONS FOR LITTLE CHILDREN FROM THE HISTORY OF THE CHURCH. By C. A. R. 1s.

LESSONS ON THE CREED. What we are to believe. 1s. 6d.

LITTLEDALE, Rev. R. F., LL.D.—Commentary on the Song of Songs. 12mo., antique cloth, 7s.

LYRA SANCTORUM; Lays for the Minor Festivals. Edited by the Rev. W. J. DEANE. 3s. 6d.

MALAN, Rev. S. C.

Bethany, a Pilgrimage; and Magdala, a Day by the Sea of Galilee. 1s. 6d.

The Coasts of Tyre and Sidon. A Narrative. 1s.

MINISTRY OF CONSOLATION, The. A Guide to Confession, for the use of Members of the Church in England. Second edition. Limp cloth, 1s. 4d.

PARISH AND THE PRIEST, The. Colloquies on the Pastoral Care, and Parochial Institutions, of a Country Village. Fcap. 8vo., 2s. 6d.

PHIPPS, Rev. J. E.—Catechism on the Holy Scriptures. 18mo., 1s.

A PRESBYTERIAN CLERGYMAN LOOKING FOR THE CHURCH. (Abridged.) 12mo., cloth, 2s.

READING LESSONS FROM SCRIPTURE HISTORY, for the Use of Schools. Royal 18mo., limp cloth, 6d.

READINGS FROM HOLY SCRIPTURE. By the Author of "Tales of Kirkbeck." First Series, 1s. 6d.; Second Series, 2s.

SCRIPTURE READING LESSONS FOR LITTLE CHIL-DREN. With a Preface by the late Bishop of Winchester. 2s. 6d.

SELECTIONS, NEW AND OLD. With a Preface by the late Bishop of Winchester. Fcap. 8vo., 4s. 6d.

SENTENCES from the Works of the Author of "Amy Herbert," selected by permission. 2s.

SPIRIT OF THE CHURCH, The. A Selection of Articles from the *Ecclesiastic*. Post 8vo. (Pub. 7s. 6d.) *Reduced to 3s. 6d.*

SPIRITUAL VOICES FROM THE MIDDLE AGES. Consisting of a Selection of Abstracts from the Writings of the Fathers, adapted for the Hour of Meditation, and concluding with a Biographical Notice of their Lives. 3s. 6d.

TROYTE, C. A. W.—Change-Ringing. An Introduction to the Early Stages of the Art of Church or Hand Bell Ringing, for the Use of Begin-ners. Third edition. Crown 8vo., cloth, 3s. 6d.; limp, 2s. 6d. The first six chapters separately, 1s.

WALCOTT, Rev. M. E. C.—Cathedralia. A Constitutional History of Cathedrals of the Western Church. 8vo., 5s.

WATSON, Rev. A.—A Catechism on the Book of Common Prayer. 2s.

WEST, Rev. J. R.
A Short Treatise on the Holy Eucharist. Fcap. 8vo., 2s. 6d.
The Memorial before God. Crown 8vo., 9d.
Tracts on Church Principles. Cloth, 1s. 6d.
Wrawby Village Dialogues. Cloth, 1s. 6d.

PRIVATE PRAYERS.

ANDREWES, Bishop.—A Manual of Private Devotions, containing Prayers for each Day in the Week, Devotions for the Holy Communion, and for the Sick. 6d.; 9d. cloth.

BRETT, Mr. R.
The Churchman's Guide to Faith and Piety. A Manual of Instructions and Devotions. Fourth Edition. Cloth, 3s. 6d.; antique calf or plain morocco, 8s. 6d. 2 vols. cloth, 4s.; limp calf, 11s.; limp morocco, 12s. Prayers for Little Children and Young Persons. 6d.; cloth, 8d.
A Manual of Devotions for School-boys. Compiled from various sources. 6d.

CHRISTIAN SERVANT'S BOOK of Devotion, Self-Examination, and Advice. Sixth Edition, cloth 1s.

COSIN, Bishop.—A Collection of Private Devotions for the Hours of Prayer. 1s.; calf, 3s. 6d.

DEVOTIONS FOR DAILY USE. Edited by a Priest (C. L. C.) Royal 32mo., cloth extra, 1s.

8

[J. Masters & Co.,

DAY HOURS OF THE CHURCH OF ENGLAND, newly Translated and Arranged according to the Prayer Book and the Authorised Translation of the Bible. 3rd edition. Crown 8vo., wrapper, 1s.; cloth, 1s. 6d.; limp calf or morocco, 7s.

SERVICE FOR CERTAIN HOLY DAYS, The. Being a Supplement to "The Day Hours of the Church of England." Crown 8vo., 2s.

DAY OFFICE OF THE CHURCH, (The) according to the Kalendar of the Church of England; consisting of Lauds, Vespers, Prime, Terce, Sext, None, and Compline, throughout the Year. To which are added, the Order for the Administration of the Reserved Eucharist, Penance, and Unction; together with the Office of the Dead, Commendation of a Soul, divers Benedictions and Offices, and full Rubrical Directions.
A complete Edition, especially for Sisterhoods and Religious Houses. By the Editor of "The Little Hours of the Day." Crown 8vo., 4s. 6d.; cloth, red edges, 5s. 6d.; calf, 9s. 6d.; morocco, 10s. 6d.

SUPPLEMENT TO THE DAY OFFICE, 9d.

THE OFFICE OF REPARATION TO THE BLESSED SACRAMENT: for those who recite the Canonical Hours according to "The Day Office of the Church," "The Day Hours of the Church of England," or "Breviary Offices." Crown 8vo. 6d.

DIAL OF MEDITATION AND PRAYER. 2nd edition, 3d.

GRAY, Rev. W. A.—The Christian's Plain Guide. 32mo., cloth, 1s.; wrapper, 6d.

HEYGATE, Rev. W. E.
The Manual: a Book of Devotion. Eighteenth edition. Cloth limp, 1s.; boards, 1s. 3d.; roan, 1s. 6d.; cheap edition, 6d.
The Manual. Adapted for general use, 12mo., cloth, 1s. 6d.

LITTLE HOURS OF THE DAY, according to the Kalendar of the Church of England. 3s. 6d. cloth; 2s. 6d. wrapper.

MALAN, Rev. S. C.—The Pocket Book of Daily Prayers. Translated from Eastern Originals. Suited for the Waistcoat Pocket. Cloth, 6d.; roan, 1s.

PAGET, Rev. F. E.—Sursum Corda : Aids to Private Devotion. Collected from the Writings of English Churchmen. 2s. 6d. cloth.

PATHWAY OF FAITH, The, or a Manual of Instructions and Prayers. For the use of those who desire to serve God in the station of life in which He has placed them. Limp cloth, 1s.; cloth boards, 1s. 3d.

PIOUS CHURCHMAN, The: a Manual of Devotion and Spiritual Instruction. 1s. 6d.

POCKET MANUAL OF PRAYERS FOR THE HOURS. 6d. Cloth, with the Collects, 1s.

PRAYERS FOR THE SEVEN CANONICAL HOURS, together with Devotions, Acts of Contrition, Faith, Hope, and Love. 32mo. cloth, 1s.

PRIMER, (The) set forth at large with many Godly and Devout Prayers. Edited, from the Post-Reformation Recension, by the Rev. Gerard Moultrie, M.A., Vicar of South Leigh. 4th Thousand. 18mo., cloth, 3s.
THE PRIMER, printed on toned paper and rubricated, 18mo., antique cloth 5s.
THE HOURS OF THE PRIMER, Published separately for the use of individual members of a household in Family Prayer. 18mo., cloth, 1s.
HORARIUM; seu Libellus Precationum, Latinè editus. 18mo., cloth, 1s.

SMITH, Rev. T. F.— The Devout Chorister Thoughts on his Vocation, and a Manual of Devotions for his use. 32mo., cloth, 1s.

YOUNG CHURCHMAN'S MANUAL, The. Second edition. 6d.

FAMILY PRAYERS.

BOOK OF FAMILY PRAYERS, collected from the Public Liturgy of the Church of England. By the Sacrist of Durham. 2s.

BOWDLER, Rev. T.—Prayers for a Christian Household, chiefly taken from the Scriptures, from the Ancient Liturgies, and the Book of Common Prayer. Fcap. 8vo., cloth, 2s. 6d.

CARTER, Rev. T. T.—Family Prayers. 3rd edition. Cloth, 1s.

DOMESTIC OFFICES: being Morning and Evening Prayer for the Use of Families. Wrapper, 6d.; cloth, 8d.

FAMILY PRAYERS FOR THE CHILDREN OF THE CHURCH. 4d., cloth 8d.

FAMILY PRAYERS FOR THE CHRISTIAN YEAR, together with Collects, with Versicles and Responses. 1s. 2d. wrapper, 1s. 6d. roan.

MONSELL.—Prayers and Litanies, taken from Holy Scripture; together with a Calendar and table of Lessons. Arranged by the Rev. J. S. B. Monsell, LL.D. 16mo., cloth, 1s.

SHORT SERVICES FOR DAILY USE IN FAMILIES. Cloth, 1s.

SUCKLING, Rev. R. A.—Family Prayers adapted to the course of the Ecclesiastical Year. 6d.; cloth, 1s.

FOR THE SICK AND AFFLICTED.

BRETT, Mr. R.
Devotions for the Sick Room, Prayers in Sickness, &c. Cloth, 2s. 6d.
Companion for the Sick Room : being a Compendium of Christian Doctrine. 2s. 6d. These two bound together in 1 vol. cloth, price 5s.
Offices for the Sick and Dying. Reprinted from the above. 1s.
Leaflets for the Sick and Dying; supplementary to the Offices for the same in "The Churchman's Guide to Faith and Piety." First Series. Price per set of eight, 6d., cardboard, 9d.
Instructions, Prayers, and Holy Aspirations for the Sick Room. 4d., cloth 6d.

BROWN, Rev. R. C. L.—The Dead in Christ. A Word of Consolation to Mourners. Super-royal 32mo., cloth, 1s. 6d.

MANUAL FOR MOURNERS, with Devotions, Directions, and Forms of Self-Examination. Fcap. 8vo., 2s. 6d.

PRAYERS AND MAXIMS, in large type, 2s.

WILKINSON, Rev. J. B.—The Hour of Death. A Manual of Prayers and Meditations intended chiefly for those in Sorrow or in Sickness. Royal 32mo., 2s.

EUCHARISTIC MANUALS.

AN ALTAR BOOK FOR YOUNG PERSONS. Suitable also for Choristers. Cloth, with a picture of the Crucifixion, 8d.; with 9 pictures, 1s. 3d.; do. red edges, gold lettered, 1s. 6d.

DEVOTIONS FOR HOLY COMMUNION. Edited by the Rev. W. U. Richards. 32mo., cloth, 1s.

EUCHARISTIC DEVOTIONS, with Preparations and Thanksgivings for Young Persons Unconfirmed or not Communicating. Royal 32mo., cloth, 9d. A companion book to "The Devout Chorister," and may be had bound with it, 1s. 6d. cloth.

10

GUIDE TO THE EUCHARIST. Containing Instructions and Directions with Forms of Preparation and Self-Examination. 4d.

HOLY EUCHARIST, The. A Manual containing Directions and suitable Devotions for those who remain in Church but do not Communicate. By a Parish Priest. 0d.

MALAN, Rev. S. C.
Prayers and Thanksgivings for the Holy Communion, chiefly for the use of the Clergy. Translated from Coptic, Armenian, and other Eastern Rituals. 1s. 6d. cloth.
Preparation for Holy Communion of the Body and Blood of CHRIST, with Prayers and Thanksgivings for the same; chiefly for the use of the Laity. Gathered and translated from Armenian and other Eastern Originals. 1s. 6d. cloth.

MANUAL FOR COMMUNICANTS: being an Assistant to a Devout and Worthy Reception of the LORD'S Supper. Roan, 1s. ; paper cover, 6d. In large type, 6d.

PRYNNE, Rev. G. R.—Eucharistic Manual, consisting of Instructions and Devotions for the Holy Sacrament of the Altar. From various sources. 1s. 6d., cloth; calf, 4s. 6d. ; morocco, 5s. Cheap edition, limp cloth, 1s. ; roan, 2s. 6d.

SCUDAMORE, Rev. W. E.
Steps to the Altar: a Manual of Devotion for the Blessed Eucharist. 51st edition. Royal 32mo., cloth, 2s.; calf or morocco, 4s. 6d. Demy 18mo., cloth, 1s ; calf or morocco, 3s. 6d.; roan, 2s. 6d. Imperial 32mo., cloth, 6d. Imitation morocco, 1s. 3d.
Incense for the Altar. A Series of Devotions for the Use of earnest Communicants, whether they receive frequently or at longer intervals. Royal 32mo., cloth, 2s. 6d. ; limp calf, 5s.

SHIPLEY. Rev. O.
The Divine Liturgy. A Manual of Devotions for the Sacrament of the Altar. Fourth Edition. Limp cloth, 1s. 6d. Superior Edition, cloth boards, 2s. 6d.
The Daily Sacrifice: a Manual of Spiritual Communion. From Ancient Sources. Limp cloth, 1s. ; cloth extra, 1s. 6d.

DEVOTIONAL BOOKS.

BELLARMINE.—The Seven Words from the Cross. A Devotional Commentary. By Bellarmine. 1s. 6d.

BRETT, Mr. R.
Reflections, Meditations, and Prayers, on the Holy Life and Passion of our LORD. New edition, 5s.
Devout Prayers on the Life and Passion of the LORD JESUS, by which the faithful soul may increase in the Love of GOD. 8d., cloth 1s.
Fervent Aspirations after Divine Love and Thanksgivings on the Passion. Part II. of the above, cloth 8d., wrapper, 6d.

COMMUNION WITH GOD. Meditations and Prayers for One Week. By a Clergyman. Fcap. 8vo., cloth, 2s.

DIVINE MASTER, The: a Devotional Manual illustrating the Way of the Cross. With Ten Steel Engravings. 9th edition, 2s. 6d. ; morocco 5s. ; antique calf or morocco 7s. Cheap edition in wrapper, 1s.

HEYGATE, Rev. W. E.
The Wedding Gift. A Devotional Manual for the Married, or those intending to Marry. 2nd edition, revised and enlarged. 3s.

A FEW DEVOTIONAL HELPS FOR THE CHRISTIAN SEASONS. Royal 32mo. 2 Vols., cloth 5s. 6d.

HIDDEN LIFE, The. Translated from Nepveu's Pensées Chrétiennes. 3rd edition, enlarged. 18mo. 2s.

HOLY CHILD JESUS. Thoughts and Prayers on the Holy Infancy and Childhood of our Blessed LORD and SAVIOUR, JESUS CHRIST. With 8 Engravings. 1s. 6d. cloth; 1s. wrapper; morocco, 4s.

HOLY CHILDHOOD OF OUR BLESSED LORD. Meditations for a Month. By the Author of "Tales of Kirkbeck." 6d.

KEMPIS.—The Soliloquy of the Soul, and the Garden of Roses. Translated from Thomas à Kempis. By the Rev. W. B. FLOWER, B.A. 2s.; cheap edition, 1s.

MALAN, Rev. S. C.
Meditations on our LORD's Passion. Translated from the Armenian of Matthew, Vartabed. 2s. 6d.
Companion for Lent. Being an Exhortation to Repentance, from the Syriac of S. Ephraem; and Thoughts for every Day in Lent, gathered from other Eastern Fathers and Divines. 1s. 3d.

MISERERE: the Fifty-first Psalm. With Devotional Notes. Reprinted from Neale's "Commentary on the Psalms." With additions by the Rev. R. F. LITTLEDALE, LL.D. 6d.; cloth, 1s.

MOULTRIE, Rev. G.
Hymns and Lyrics, for the Seasons and Saints' Days of the Church. Fcap. 8vo., 6s.
Offices for Holy Week and Easter, after the Primer Use, together with the Meditations on the Life and Passion of our LORD. Edited by the Rev. G. MOULTRIE, M.A. 18mo. 3s.

OUR NEW LIFE IN CHRIST. Edited by a Parish Priest, C. L. C. Fourth edition. 18mo., cloth, 1s.; cheap edition, 6d.

A SEQUEL TO "OUR NEW LIFE IN CHRIST;" OR, THE PRESENCE OF JESUS ON THE ALTAR. With a Few Simple Ways of Worshipping Him at the Celebration of the Blessed Sacrament. To which are added, Devotions and Hymns. 18mo., limp cloth, 1s.; cloth boards, red edges, 1s. 6d.

PAGET, Rev. F. E.—The Christian's Day. Royal 32mo., 2s. cloth.

PEOPLE'S HYMNAL, The, containing 600 Hymns, Carols, and Metrical Litanies. Wrapper, 6d.; limp cloth, 8d.; cloth boards, red edges, 1s.; roan, red edges, 1s. 9d. Large Type edition, cloth boards, 2s.; roan, 4s.

PRACTICAL SCIENCE OF THE CROSS IN THE USE OF THE SACRAMENTS OF PENANCE AND THE EUCHARIST. By M. the Abbé GROU. Translated from the French. 18mo., cloth. 2s. 6d.; wrapper, 2s.

PRACTICE OF THE PRESENCE OF GOD THE BEST RULE OF A HOLY LIFE, being Conversations and Letters of Brother Lawrence. Sixth edition. Royal 32mo, 4d.; cloth, 6d.; morocco, 1s. 6d.

PSALTER, The; or Seven Ordinary Hours of Prayer, according to the use of the Church of Sarum. Beautifully printed and bound in antique parchment. Reduced to 15s.

SHIPLEY, The Rev. Orby.
Eucharistic Meditations for a Month on the Most Holy Communion. Translated from the French of Avrillon. Limp cloth, 2s. 6d.
Daily Meditations: from Ancient Sources. Edited by the Rev. Orby Shipley Advent to Easter. Cloth, 1s. 6d.
Daily Meditations for a Month, on some of the more moving truths of Christianity; in order to determine the Soul to be in earnest in the love and service of her GOD. From ancient sources. Edited by the Rev. Orby Shipley. Cloth, 1s.
A Treatise of the Virtue of Humility, abridged from the Spanish of Rodriguez; for the use of persons living in the world. Cloth, 1s.
Considerations on Mysteries of the Faith, newly translated and abridged from the Original Spanish of Luis de Granada. 2s. cloth.
Spiritual Exercises: Readings for a Retreat of Seven Days. Translated and abridged from the French of Bourdaloue. Edited by the Rev. Orby Shipley. 1s. 6d.

THREE HOURS AGONY: Meditations, Prayers, and Hymns on the Seven Words from the Cross of our Most Holy Redeemer, together with Additional Devotions on the Passion. Fourteenth Thousand. 4d.

TUTE, Rev. J. S.—Meditations on the Most Precious Blood and Example of CHRIST. Fcap. 8vo., cloth, 1s. 6d.

VERSES FOR THE SUNDAYS AND HOLIDAYS OF THE CHRISTIAN YEAR. By the Author of the "Daily Life of the Christian Child," &c., with Illustrations. 2s.

WILLIAMS, The late Rev. I.
The Altar; or Meditations in Verse on the Holy Communion. By the author of "The Cathedral." 2s. 6d.
Hymns on the Catechism. 6d., cloth 1s.

BOOKS FOR THE USE OF THE CLERGY.

THE PRIEST'S PRAYER BOOK, with a brief Pontifical. Containing Private Prayers and Intercessions; Offices, Readings, Prayers, Litanies, and Hymns, for the Visitation of the Sick; Offices for Bible and Confirmation Classes, Cottage Lectures, &c.; Notes on Confession, Direction, Missions, and Retreats; Remedies for Sin; Anglican Orders; Bibliotheca Sacerdotalis, &c., &c. EDITED BY TWO CLERGYMEN. Fifth Edition, much enlarged. *Reprinting.*

THE CLERGYMAN'S MANUAL OF PRIVATE PRAYERS. Collected and Compiled from Various Sources. A Companion Book to "The Priest's Prayer Book." Cloth, 1s.

HORARIUM; seu Libellus Precationum, Latinè editus. 18mo., cloth, 1s.

MEMORIALE VITÆ SACERDOTALIS; or, Solemn Warnings of the Great Shepherd, JESUS CHRIST, to the Clergy of His Holy Church. From the Latin of Arvisenet. Adapted to the Use of the English Church by the BISHOP OF BRECHIN. Second edition. Fcap. 8vo., cloth, 3s. 6d.

THE PRIEST IN HIS INNER LIFE. By H. P. L. 1s.

HEYGATE, Rev. W. E.—Ember Hours. New edition, revised, with an Essay on RELIGION IN RELATION TO SCIENCE, by the Rev. T. S. ACKLAND, M.A., Vicar of Balne, author of "Story of Creation," &c. Fcap. 8vo., cloth, 3s.

OWEN, Rev. R.—An Introduction to the Study of Dogmatic Theology. 8vo., 12s.

PAGET, Rev. F. E.
Memoranda Parochialia; or, the Parish Priest's Pocket Book. 3s. 6d.; double size 5s.
Sermons for Special Occasions. Containing Twenty-one Sermons for Consecration of Churches, Churchyards, Restoration, Anniversary, Foundation Stone, New School, School Feast, Confirmation, Ordination, Visitation, Church and Educational Societies, Choirs, Wakes, Festivals, Clubs, and Assizes. Post 8vo., 5s.

SERMONS REGISTER, for Ten Years, by which an account may be kept of Sermons, the number, subject, and when preached. Post 4to., 1s.

REGISTER OF SERMONS, PREACHERS, NUMBER OF COMMUNICANTS, AND AMOUNT OF OFFERTORY. Fcap. 4to., roan, 4s. 6d. (The Book of Strange Preachers as ordered by the 52nd Canon.)

REGISTER OF PERSONS CONFIRMED AND ADMITTED TO HOLY COMMUNION. For 500 names, 4s. 6d. For 1000 names, 7s. 6d., half-bound.

THE LITANY from the Book of Common Prayer, together with the latter part of the COMMINATION SERVICE, with Musical Notation throughout for Priest, Choir, and People. Edited by RICHARD REDHEAD. Demy 4to. Handsomely printed in red and black. Wrapper, 7s. 6d.; imitation morocco, 18s.; morocco plain, 24s.; morocco panelled, &c., 30s.

THOMPSON, Rev. H.
Concionalia; Outlines of Sermons for Parochial Use throughout the Year. First Series. Third edition. Fcap. 8vo., 7s. 6d.
Concionalia. Second Series. Fcap. 8vo., 6s. 6d.

BARING GOULD, Rev. S.
One Hundred Sketches of Sermons for Extempore Preachers. Second Edition. Crown 8vo., 6s.
Village Conferences on the Creed. Crown 8vo., 3s. 6d.

SERMONS AND LECTURES.

ASHLEY, Rev. J. M.
The Victory of the Spirit: a Course of Short Sermons by way of Commentary on the Eighth Chapter of S. Paul's Epistle to the Romans. Fcap. 8vo., cloth, 2s.
Thirteen Sermons from the Quaresimale of Quirico Rossi. Translated from the Italian. Edited by J. M. ASHLEY, B.C.L. Fcap. 8vo., cloth, 3s. 6d.

BAINES, Rev. J.—Sermons. Fcap. 8vo. cloth, 5s.

BRIGHT, Rev. Canon, D.D.—Eighteen Sermons of S. Leo the Great on the Incarnation, translated with Notes and with the "Tome" of S. Leo in the original. 8vo., cloth, 5s.

BUTLER, Rev. W. J.—Sermons for Working Men. Second edition. 12mo., 6s. 6d.

CHAMBERS, Rev. J. C.—Fifty-two Sermons preached at Perth and in other parts of Scotland. 8vo., 12s.

[J. Masters & Co.,

CHAMBERLAIN, Rev. T.
The Theory of Christian Worship. Second edition. 3s. 6d.
The Seven Ages of the Church as indicated in the Messages to the Seven
Churches of Asia. Post 8vo., 3s.

CHANTER, Rev. J. M.—Sermons. 12mo., 3s. 6d.

CODD, Rev. E. T.—Sermons addressed to a Country Congregation, in-
cluding Four preached before the University of Cambridge. Third Series.
12mo., 6s. 6d.

CHEYNE, Rev. P.
The Teaching of the Christian Year: a Series of Sermons. Vol. I., Ad-
vent to Whitsuntide. 7s.
The Consolations of the Cross; and the Rest of the Blessed. Fcap.
8vo., 2s.
Six Sermons on the Holy Eucharist. 8vo., 2s.

DAVIDSON, Rev. J. P. F.—The Holy Communion. A Course of Sermons preached in the Parish Church of Chipping Sodbury. Fcap. 8vo.,
2s. 6d.

DAVIES, Rev. G.—Benefit Club Sermons. 1st and 2nd Series. In one
Vol. Second edition. 4to., 3s.

EVANS, Rev. A. B., D.D.—Christianity in its Homely Aspects: Sermons on Various Subjects. Second Series. 12mo., 3s.

FLOWER, Rev. W. B.—Sermons for the Seasons of the Church,
translated from S. Bernard. 8vo., 6s.

FORD, Rev. J.
Sermons from the Quaresimale of P. Paolo Segneri. 8vo., 3 vols. 6s.
each. In One Vol. 15s.
Twelve Sermons preached in the Chapel of Liverydole Almshouse at
Heavitree. 12mo., 3s.

GALTON, Rev. J. L.
One Hundred and Forty-two Lectures on the Book of Revelation. In
Two Vols. Fcap. 8vo., 18s.
Notes of Lectures on the Book of Canticles or Song of Solomon, delivered
in the Parish Church of S. Sidwell, Exeter. 6s.

GRESLEY, Rev. W.
Practical Sermons. 12mo., 3s. 6d.
Sermons preached at Brighton. 12mo., 3s. 6d.

HAMILTON, Rev. L. R.—Parochial Sermons. Fcap. 8vo., 3s. 6d.

IRONS, Rev. W. J., D.D.
The Preaching of CHRIST. A Series of Sixty Sermons for the People. In
a packet, 5s., cloth, 6s.
The Miracles of CHRIST: being a Second Series of Sermons for the People.
Second edition. 8vo., 6s.

LEA, Rev. W.—Sermons on the Prayer Book. Fcap. 8vo., 2s.

LEE, Rev. F. G., D.C.L.
Miscellaneous Sermons, by Clergymen of the Church of England. Edited
by F. G. Lee. Crown 8vo., 3s. 6d.
The Message of Reconciliation. In Four Sermons. 8vo., 2s.

MILLARD, Rev. F. M.—S. Peter's Denial of CHRIST. Seven short
Sermons to Boys. Fcap. 8vo., 1s. 4d.

MOUNTAIN, Rev. J. H. B., D.D.—Sermons for the Seasons, and on other occasions. 8vo., 3s. 6d.

NEWLAND, Rev. H.—Postils; Short Sermons on the Parables, &c., adapted from the Fathers. Second edition. Fcap. 8vo., 3s.

NUGEE, Rev. G.—The Words from the Cross as applied to our own Deathbeds. Second edition. Fcap. 8vo., 2s. 6d.

PAGET, Rev. F. E.
Sermons on the Saints' Days. 12mo., 3s. 6d.
Sermons for Special Occasions. Crown 8vo., 5s.

PRICHARD, Rev. J. C.—Sermons. Fcap. 8vo., 4s 6d.

PRYNNE, Rev. G. R.
Plain Parochial Sermons. Second Series. 8vo., 10s. 6d.
Parochial Sermons. (New Volume.) 8vo. cloth, 10s. 6d.

POTT, The Ven. Archdeacon.
Confirmation Lectures delivered to a Village Congregation in the Diocese of Oxford. Third edition. 2s.
Village Lectures on the Sacraments and Occasional Services of the Church. 2s.

SERMONS by various Contributors illustrating the Offices of the Prayer Book. 8vo., 3s. 6d.

STRETTON, Rev. H.—The Acts of S. Mary Magdalene considered in Sixteen Sermons. 8vo., 5s.

SUCKLING, Rev. R. A.—Sermons Plain and Practical. Fourth edit. Fcap. 8vo., 3s. 6d.

TOMLINS, Rev. R.—Sermons for the Greater Cycle of High Days in the Church's Year, with Sermons for Special and Ordinary Occasions. Second edition. 12mo., 5s.

WEST, Rev. J. R.
Parish Sermons on the Chief Articles of the Christian Faith. Fcp. 8vo., 6s.
Sermons on the Ascension of our LORD. Fcap. 8vo., 3s. 6d.
Parish Sermons for the Advent and Christmas Seasons. Fcap. 8vo. 3s.

WILKINSON, Rev. J. B.
Mission Sermons. Twenty-five Plain Sermons preached in London and Country Churches and Missions. Second edition. Fcap. 8vo., 3s. 6d.
Mission Sermons. Second Series. Fcap. 8vo., 5s.
Mission Sermons. Third Series. Fcap. 8vo., 6s.

WINDSOR, Rev. S. B.—Sermons for Soldiers preached at Home and Abroad. Fcap. 8vo., 3s. 6d.

WROTH, Rev. W. R.—Five Sermons on some of the Old Testament Types of Holy Baptism. Post 8vo., 3s.

J. MASTERS AND CO., 78, NEW BOND STREET.